MONSTERSTREET

CARNEVIL

3

MONSTERSTREET

CARNEVIL

J. H. REYNOLDS

KATHERINE TEGEN BOOKS
An Imprint of HarperCollins Publishers

Library of Congress Control Number: 2019939495
ISBN 978-0-06-286941-8 (trade)
ISBN 978-0-06-286940-1 (pbk.)

Typography by Ray Shappell
19 20 21 22 23   PC/BRR   10 9 8 7 6 5 4 3 2 1

First Edition
Also available in a hardcover edition.

To Kevin Reynolds, Lee Carter, and Bob Darden—
my three mentors who gave me the courage
to keep writing

1

A STRANGE WIND

The two brothers stepped off the train, dragging their suitcases behind them. Ren was twelve, had perfectly combed hair, and wore his shirttail tucked in. Kip was nine, hadn't combed his hair in days, and wouldn't tuck in his shirt if his life depended on it.

It was their first time away from their parents for more than one night, and they had been given strict instructions to wait at the outdoor depot once they arrived at their destination. But when they looked around for somewhere to sit down, they realized that they were the only ones there.

"This place gives me the creeps," Ren said.

"Scaredy-cat," Kip replied. "What time is Aunt Winnie supposed to pick us up?"

"Four o'clock sharp," Ren said, glancing down at his watch.

A crow cawed, and the boys turned to see a flock of black birds flying away from a scarecrow in the nearby cornfield. The brittle shucks quivered as a cool October breeze swept over Ren and Kip, carrying a strange scent upon it.

"Do you smell that?" Ren asked.

"Yeah. Smells like . . . pumpkins," Kip said. "And cotton candy."

"And something else too. What is it?" Ren mused aloud.

"I don't know, but can you help me carry this?" Kip asked, tugging at his suitcase, which was twice his size.

"You're old enough to carry your own luggage," Ren said, forgetting about the scent for a moment.

"But it's too heavy," Kip complained. "And mom said you're supposed to look after me while we're here."

"Only because she doesn't want you to get in trouble like you always do," Ren said, then reluctantly helped Kip pull his suitcase to a nearby bench. "I swear, Mom and Dad should pay me for being your full-time babysitter."

"They don't pay you because brothers are *supposed* to look out for each other," Kip said. "Clay Ferguson's big brother takes him on bike rides and to get ice cream and even to the movies. They're like . . . friends."

"Well, if you weren't so annoying, maybe I'd let you tag along too," Ren replied. "Not all of us can do whatever we want when we want— there's a little thing called responsibility."

"Hey, I can be responsible," Kip said.

"Yeah right. When was the last time you made your bed or helped Mom unload the dishwasher?"

Kip didn't say anything.

"It's the same everywhere we go," Ren continued. "I have to be the responsible one while you get to have all the fun."

Kip looked at the ground, and Ren could tell he had hurt his little brother's feelings.

Just as he was about to apologize, a black hearse with tinted windows slowly rolled into the empty parking lot and stopped. Chills shot up Ren's spine as he realized that whoever was inside it was staring right at them.

2

LAND OF THE DEAD

The hearse didn't move. It just sat there with the engine still running, like a spider waiting patiently in the shadows of its web.

"Should I call the cops?" Ren whispered, eyeing the nearby pay phone. But Kip looked more curious than afraid.

Ren felt his breath quickening as he peered at the dark windshield glaring back at them.

What do they want? he wondered.

Suddenly, the engine turned off.

The driver door creaked open.

And a pair of black tennis shoes appeared.

A brown-haired woman wearing sunglasses and a nurse's uniform stepped out of the hearse and waved at them. She looked a few years younger than their mom.

"Aunt Winnie?" Ren said in disbelief.

"Hi, boys!" she called. "Sorry, I had to take a moment to touch up my makeup."

They met her at the bottom of the depot steps, and she gave them both hugs.

"I swear you two have grown a foot since last Thanksgiving! I'm so glad I get you for an entire week while your parents are away on their anniversary trip in Europe. We're going to have so much fun!"

Ren had always liked Aunt Winnie more than his other aunts and uncles. She was the only older person he knew who really seemed to care about what a kid had to say. Plus, she always sent the best birthday presents.

"What's with the hearse?" Kip asked. "Do you work for a funeral home or something?"

Aunt Winnie laughed.

"Something like that," she teased. "Let's get

your bags in the back with the coffin, and I'll take you to . . . the Land of the Dead!"

"The Land of the Dead?" Ren questioned.

But Aunt Winnie didn't explain.

As they drove through the nearby neighborhood, Ren observed Halloween décor in every yard. There were blow-up monsters and fake gravestones, smoking witch's cauldrons and light-up animatronic figures. It seemed every house in town went all out for Halloween.

All the while, the pumpkin-candy scent poured through the hearse's open windows.

"Don't you just love this time of year?" Aunt Winnie said. "I can't believe Halloween is only a few days away. Did you boys bring costumes? If not, I can throw something together for you."

"I think I'll pass," Ren said. "Every Halloween, I end up spending the entire night chasing after Kip and making sure he doesn't get in trouble."

"I can help watch Kip so that you can have fun too," Aunt Winnie replied.

"Really?" Ren asked.

"Sure," Aunt Winnie said. "I mean, we're talking about Halloween here. The one night of the year you can become anything you want! Besides, you're only a kid once."

Ren half smiled. The idea of actually getting to have fun on Halloween sounded too good to be true.

A few minutes later, Aunt Winnie turned in to a long driveway, and Ren observed the rusted iron sign above the arched stone entrance. It was overgrown with twisting green vines, but he could still make out the words *Old Manor Nursing Home*.

"You work at a nursing home?" Ren asked.

"You boys will love it," Aunt Winnie said. "It's like living in a library, only the books can talk to you. I've wanted to work here since I was in college. So when they invited me to be their activities director, I jumped at the opportunity. There's something special about helping people during their last stop in life, you know."

"Creepy is more like it," Kip mumbled.

Ren elbowed Kip in his ribs.

"That sounds nice, Aunt Winnie," Ren said, then glared at Kip and added, "and responsible."

Kip rolled his eyes.

Once inside the property grounds, Ren expected to see dozens of old people wandering around in the garden while others sat in wheelchairs staring out into nothingness. But instead, he saw pumpkins grinning from behind each window, black streamers strung above every door, and droves of elderly people cobwebbing the porch.

"Welcome to the Land of the Dead," Aunt Winnie announced.

Ren looked up and saw a giant hand-painted sign hanging over the front doors of the nursing home.

Beware . . .
You Are Now Entering the Haunted Manor!

"*This* is the Land of the Dead?" Kip asked. "Do you call it that because people die here all the time?"

"Kip!" Aunt Winnie said. "We're actually just transforming Old Manor into a big haunted house for Halloween night—the Haauuunntted Maaannnooooorrr!" she said in her spookiest voice. "I've put ads in the local gazette, inviting all the neighborhood kids to come trick-or-treating here. I even rented this hearse for the week to keep parked out front to give it extra ambience."

"You're not going to need to put much makeup on these old people for your haunted house," Kip said, then pointed to the small graveyard in the empty field next to the manor. "Everyone here already looks half-dead."

Ren nudged Kip again.

"Kip, please show a little respect while you're here," Aunt Winnie said. "These folks have lived stories beyond your wildest dreams. And as you can see, they're quite fond of Halloween. I spent half our annual activities budget at the Halloween store. Maybe you boys can help us finish decorating. There are still quite a few boxes to bring up from the basement, and I could use some help getting this coffin inside."

As the boys stepped out of the hearse, a crinkled sheet of paper twirled in the strange autumn wind and blew up against Ren's shin. He picked up the flyer and read it.

> *Experience the horror, the mystery, the wonder!*
>
> *Get your ticket to the scariest carnival in the world.*
>
> *But beware . . . you may not make it out alive.*
>
> **Bring this flyer to the Carnival of Horrors for one free ride!*

Ren looked up and saw a giant black Ferris Wheel looming in the distance, reaching toward the gray October sky. The wheel was surrounded by a tiny village of orange-and-black-striped tents and rusty rides, all dotted with alluring purple lights. At the sight of it all, Ren realized what the peculiar scent had been.

The carnival! he thought. *With its funnel cakes and cotton candy, turkey legs and roasted corn, and a thousand other autumn delights . . .*

But there had been something else in the scent too—something he still couldn't name.

Aunt Winnie stepped out of the car and noticed the flyer in Ren's hand.

"You know, it's weird," she said. "I woke up this morning, and that Halloween carnival had just appeared overnight. No trains. No trucks. Nothing. It's like it conjured itself out of thin air."

3

ZOMBIE MANOR

As soon as Ren stepped through the mausoleum-themed doors of the nursing home, the sweet scents of the carnival collided with the smells of bleach and floor wax.

"You boys can have your own room in the guest house. I'll be just down the hall from you," Aunt Winnie said, pointing out a window to a small house beside Old Manor.

Ren and Kip peered down a dimly lit hallway. Several old people were hanging up black streamers across the walls, the soles of their slippers squeaking against the floors.

"They look like zombies," Kip whispered to Ren. "Do you think they'll try to eat our brains while we're asleep?"

"First you'd have to have brains for them to eat," Ren said.

Just then, a high-pitched beeping sound pierced their ears, and Ren noticed a red light blinking on the giant service board behind the front desk.

"Geesh. Where is Brad when I need him?" Aunt Winnie said.

"Who's Brad?" Ren asked.

"He's the head nurse," Aunt Winnie replied, examining the service board. Her eyes suddenly filled with dread. "Oh no, not Room 1942. Any room but 1942."

She turned to Ren.

"Can you do me a favor and go check on Mrs. Wellshire?"

"Why me?"

"Because all the other nurses are busy, and I— Well, let's just say Mrs. Wellshire hasn't taken to me very well. She's already thrown three trays at me this week," Aunt Winnie said. Ren wondered how anyone couldn't like his aunt. "I'll give you boys twenty dollars to go to the carnival later if you just do this one favor for me."

Kip began jumping up and down with excitement.

"Oh, please, Ren!" he begged. "I've never been to a carnival! Please, pretty please!"

Ren looked down at his little brother. The only other time he had seen Kip so excited was when their parents had given him his first bike.

"All right, all right," Ren surrendered. "But only if you don't annoy me the rest of the time we're here."

"No problem!" Kip promised.

"Mrs. Wellshire's room is just down that way," Aunt Winnie said, pointing Ren in the right direction. "I'll help Kip carry your bags to your room. When you're done, come back here and give me an update. Then I'll drop you boys off at the carnival."

Reluctantly, Ren started down the hallway,

counting down the room numbers posted beside the doors decorated like coffin lids. . . .

"1962 . . . 1961 . . . 1960 . . . 1959 . . ."

Several doors were open, revealing glimpses of the residents in each room.

Some sat watching Halloween movies in front of buzzing TVs.

Others were decorating their walls with skeleton and gargoyle cutouts.

A few were even crafting their own costumes.

All the while, Ren tried to ignore the smells of bleach and Lysol that lingered in the air.

When he finally arrived at Room 1942, the door was cracked open, and the room was as dark as midnight. In fact, it was the only room on the hall that didn't have a single Halloween decoration outside it.

Knock, knock.

No one answered.

Ren gently pushed open the door and saw a tray of uneaten food sitting on a table beside the bed.

Then he noticed someone sleeping in the bed, covered in a mound of blankets.

"Mrs. Wellshire, I just came by to see if you needed anything," he called out, stepping inside the room.

Still no answer.

What if she's dead? Ren thought, wondering how cold her corpse might be.

The possibility chilled him.

He gulped.

Then cautiously, he reached to pull back the blanket. . . .

4

OUT OF THE DARKNESS

Maybe I should go get Aunt Winnie, he mused, having second thoughts.

But curiosity overcame him.

Slowly, he pulled back the blanket and cringed at the sight of the stuffed, disfigured thing beneath it.

A pillow?

Ren laughed, feeling both silly and relieved.

He turned to exit, deciding Mrs. Wellshire must have left her room. But he stopped when he heard a frightened voice creep out of the darkness. . . .

"H-have they left? Is it safe now?"

Ren squinted and saw a twisted figure crouching in the closet, veiled in shadow.

"H-has who left?" he called back.

"The carnies," the voice returned, and a withered face leaned into the dusty light pouring in from the hallway. "I heard them come in the night."

The old woman with frizzy white hair stepped out of the closet, and Ren noticed her hands were trembling. She was so pale, he could see the tangle of blue veins beneath her skin.

"I woke up in the night and saw the purple haze out my window. And the tents," she said. "Just like last time. We were warned to stay away, but we didn't listen. And now they're back. For another harvest."

She reached down and touched the odd-shaped scar on her forearm.

"What are you talking about?" Ren asked.

But Mrs. Wellshire didn't answer. Instead, she began pacing back and forth, babbling things that Ren couldn't understand.

When she noticed the flyer in his hand, she grabbed it eagerly and examined it, as if looking for a hidden message.

"Hey, give that back!" Ren said. "I need it to get a free ride!"

He took the flyer and glared at the old woman. She seemed haunted by something.

"I—I just came to see if you needed anything," Ren explained. "My aunt is the director here and asked me to come check on you."

He stepped backward toward the door, keeping an eye on the old woman. She stood in the same place, but turned her shoulders squarely toward him.

"Whatever you do, don't listen to him," she warned. "Everything he says is a candy-coated lie."

"Everything who says?" Ren asked.

"The Tick-Tock Man," Mrs. Wellshire whispered.

Ren didn't know why, but his blood turned cold at the mention of the name.

This place is getting in my head. I've got to get

out of here, he thought.

Ren stepped out of the room and closed the door, leaving Mrs. Wellshire alone in the dark.

He waited outside her room for a moment, listening to see if she was going to come after him. But the door remained sealed.

No wonder Aunt Winnie didn't want to come down here, he thought, then looked at the balled-up flyer in his hand. *Carnivals show up in lots of towns this time of year. It can't be that bad.*

But by the end of the night, he would think otherwise.

5

CARNIVAL OF HORRORS

Aunt Winnie pulled up in front of the carnival gates and handed a twenty-dollar bill to Ren.

"Make sure you split this equally. And stay together at all times, okay? I'll pick you boys up at this same spot in two hours."

Ren nodded, then he and Kip climbed out of the car.

They waved goodbye as Aunt Winnie drove onto the main road back toward Old Manor. As soon as she was out of sight, Kip pulled his blue baseball cap tight over his shaggy hair and sprinted toward the gates.

"Hey, wait up!" Ren yelled, chasing after him.

Ren zigzagged in and out of the crowd, shoving his way through the bat-wing entrance to catch up to Kip.

Once inside, their eyes filled with wonder.

This carnival wasn't like other carnivals.

It wasn't like anything they'd ever seen.

It was . . .

A Halloween wonderland!

Everywhere they looked, festive marvels glared back at them.

Flickering jack-o'-lanterns blazed at the entrance of every ride. Costumed carnies handed out candy from ghoulish pumpkin buckets. And creepy music played from some unseen calliope while a cloud of bats circled overhead, as if waiting to feast on something dead below.

It felt like being on the set of a spooky Halloween movie.

Nearby, a carnival barker in a cobwebbed top hat and tarantula-infested jacket shouted at the passing crowd, "Come one! Come all! Welcome to the scariest carnival in the world, where you can experience all the thrills, chills, and horrors your heart desires! We have Clowntown and the Haunted Mirror Maze, the Jaws of Death and the Drop of Fear, brain-fried funnel cakes and blood-soaked cotton candy! Be afraid—yes, be very afraid—for this is your death rehearsal!"

Kip gazed around wide-eyed at all of it, as if he had just entered a bizarre, delicious dream.

"Let's ride every ride and eat every kind of spooky food they have!" he shouted.

"We have to pace ourselves," Ren warned, looking around for anyone that might resemble a Tick-Tock Man. "Twenty dollars should get us each something to eat and a few rides."

Ren walked over to the nearby ticket booth and traded in the money for twenty tickets. When he counted to make sure the ticket operator had given him enough for his money, he saw that each ticket had the silhouette of a bat printed on it.

"Which ride do you want to do first?" he asked Kip.

"That one!" Kip said, pointing to the tallest

ride at the very back of the carnival.

Ren watched from afar as one by one, kids lay down in a wooden coffin, were pulled two hundred feet in the air on rickety tracks, and then free-fell into a giant grave carved into the ground. A smoke machine blew up a cloud of fog after each coffin disappeared into the black cavity.

The neon sign at the entrance read:

Drop of Fear

"No way. I'm not doing that one," Ren replied. "And I'm not doing Clowntown either. You know how much I hate clowns."

"Then I'll do it alone," Kip said, starting toward the ride.

Ren grabbed his arm.

"Aunt Winnie told me not to let you out of my sight," Ren reminded. "So whatever rides we do, we do them together."

Kip pulled his arm away from Ren. "But you're afraid of everything! If we do that, we won't end up riding any of them!"

"I'm not afraid. Just . . . cautious. Anyway, that ride looks like it could collapse any day now," Ren said, then pointed to the rickety tracks, rusted from years of autumn thrills.

"So what if it does—what if you're standing beneath it because you were too afraid to get on? And then you get crushed by your own fear?"

Ren realized that he had imagined all the bad things that could happen to him if he got on to the ride, but he had never considered the bad things that could happen to him if he didn't.

"Let's just find something else," Ren said.

Annoyed but not wanting to miss out on a second of fun, Kip ran to get in line for the Skeleton Coaster. Ren followed after him and handed two tickets to the carnie operating it.

For the next hour, Ren followed Kip around the carnival as he rode ride after ride. Ren even gave up one of his own tickets so Kip could ride the Ghost Ship a second time.

Afterward, Kip hurried to a food stand and

ordered a brain-fried funnel cake and a skull-shaped souvenir cup filled with liver-flavored lemonade.

"I guess this is what they do with all the kids who fall off the rides. The ones who go *splat*! They grind them up and feed them back to the customers," Kip said, then took a giant bite of his funnel cake.

"You're demented, you know that? Those are just the names they give the food to go along with the theme of the carnival. It's not really brain-fried or liver-flavored."

"How can you be so sure?" Kip asked just to annoy Ren.

Ren shook his head in frustration.

"You know, you might be the most irritating little brother on the face of the planet," he said.

"All right, all right. How many tickets do we have left?" Kip asked, then slurped a sip of lemonade.

Ren felt in his pockets.

"None," he said. "We're out."

"What do you mean?" Kip asked.

"I mean we don't have any left. We wouldn't have run out so fast if you had paced yourself like I told you," Ren said. "You should try listening to me sometime."

"What about that?" Kip asked, pointing to Ren's back pocket. Ren reached down and pulled out the flyer.

"I almost forgot," he said. "We get one free ride with this."

"Ha, I knew it!" Kip shouted, and started to look around at their options.

The Spider Spin was just across the midway next to the Witch's Cauldron. But a Halloween Freak Show tent loomed to their left. The side of the canvas tent displayed drawings of a two-headed werewolf named Fang, a four-legged woman named Scary Mary, and an impossible creature with a jack-o'-lantern head called Johnny Pumpkinhead.

The boys' only other options nearby were the Cobwebbed Carousel or the Twisted Ventriloquist Show, where supposedly the puppets and humans switched places.

"Which one should I use my flyer for?"

"*Your* flyer? It blew up against *my* leg," Ren said. "Besides, you used over half of our tickets."

"But I'm the youngest," Kip said.

"And I'm the oldest," Ren replied.

Just then, a girl's voice interrupted them.

"Tell you what—how about I read both your fortunes for that one flyer?"

They turned and saw a girl wearing a black dress and a purple sash wrapped around her head. Two spider-shaped earrings hung from her ears, and her emerald eyes were framed with black eyeliner, giving her the look of a gothic enchantress. Weirdly, even though she looked their age, she had several streaks of gray hair.

"You mean you'll read our fortunes for free?" Ren asked.

"Nothing's free at the carnival," she said, then gestured for them to enter her tent. "Consider this a discount."

"Awesome!" Kip said, hurrying into the tent without giving it a second thought. Ren followed.

"I'm Zora," she said, offering her hand.

"I'm Ren. And this is my little brother, Kip."

They both shook her hand.

Ren glanced around and saw that Zora's tent was lined with black satin, giving it a dark appearance, like something out of an old horror film. Two chairs sat side by side at her table, as if she had been expecting the boys.

They sat down, and Kip immediately touched the moon-colored ball at the center of the table. Purple lightning zapped toward his finger, giving him a mild shock.

"Wow. Magic," Kip said in awe.

"It's just an illusion," Ren whispered. "There's no such thing as real magic."

Zora smirked knowingly as she fed her pet spiders beneath the table. Then she sat down and spoke an incantation of indecipherable words.

When she finished, the crystal ball floated off the table and hovered in midair.

6

MOONY VISIONS

Ren watched as the ball began to glow, dissolving the darkness around it. He waved his hand over and beneath it to see if there were any strings attached. But he couldn't feel any.

Kip, on the other hand, was hypnotized by the trick.

Zora continued her spell, moving her hands majestically in front of the ball, as if trying to awaken some sleeping thing within it. Soon, the ball filled with fog, and a cryptic vision appeared.

"I will gaze into my haunted ball and tell you what I see in your futures," she began.

The girl peered deeper into the mystical orb, and Ren and Kip scooted closer to get a better look.

"I see two figures, two boys," she continued. "One of them is wearing a mask, and the other is wearing . . . two masks."

"What does that mean?" Ren asked.

"Only the oracle knows," Zora said mysteriously. "And now I see a clock . . . yes, a clock . . . that turns backward," Zora said.

"A clock that turns backward?" Kip asked. "I've never seen anything like that."

"There are many marvels in the world you have yet to see, boy," she replied, which Ren thought was weird because she wasn't any older than them.

Zora continued consulting the ball, and a stream of images reeled through it. Ren and Kip waited patiently for her next revelation.

Soon, the ball turned solid black, and Zora's eyes grew distressed.

"The oracle has sent a warning: it says, 'The bond of love repels evil, but a love-bond broken invites evil in.'"

"What does that mean?" Ren asked.

"It means your chances of survival are better if you stick together," Zora said.

Ren and Kip exchanged a worried look.

Zora then saw something else in the ball that the boys couldn't see. She squinted, as if concerned, then quickly turned and opened her ancient spell book. She flipped through the pages, as if searching for an answer. She stopped on a page in the middle of the book and ran her finger over its text.

After a moment, she looked up at them.

"What is it?" Ren asked.

She closed the book and leaned forward, as if she didn't want anyone else to hear. "You both need to leave the carnival right now and never come back."

"Why?" Ren asked, still not fully believing her magic was real but believing just enough to be afraid.

Zora took a deep breath and let it out slowly. "According to the vision, one of you is going to—"

She paused.

"Going to what?" Ren asked.

But Zora seemed distracted. Ren realized that she was no longer looking at her moon-ball but rather behind them toward the entrance of her tent.

Curious, Ren slowly turned . . . and saw . . .

A man in a black cape.

Holding a wooden cane crowned by a ticking clock.

7

BROTHER'S KEEPER

"Good evening, Zora," the man said in a deep, charming voice.

Zora lowered the moon-ball to the table. She looked caught off guard, like a kid who was in trouble.

"I was just—I was just looking into these boys' futures," Zora explained.

"Find anything interesting?" the man asked, stepping toward them.

"Fame and riches," she lied, feigning a smile. "These boys are the lucky sort."

The man picked up a gold coin from the

table and rolled it over his knuckles.

"Destiny is a strange thing—there are always two sides to every coin . . . to every choice," he said. "One leads to life, and the other . . . to death."

He closed his palm around the coin, and when he opened it again, the coin had vanished.

"Wooow," Kip said. "You're a magician?"

"Of a sort," the man replied with a slight grin. He turned as if he was about to leave but stopped just behind Kip. "Oh, and . . . if you boys like magic, be sure to come to the big show on Halloween night."

"The big show?" Kip asked.

The man nodded. "You won't want to miss it. It will be to die for."

Something about the way he said the last sentence made Ren feel uncomfortable.

"W-we're just visiting town," Ren said, not wanting Kip to get too friendly with the stranger. "And we ran out of tickets. I don't think our aunt is going to give us more money to come back."

"Ah, did Zora not tell you?" the man replied.

"There are other ways to pay for the rides."

He raised his cane in parting. When he turned back toward the entrance, his cape made a ruffling sound in the air.

As soon as he disappeared out of the tent, Zora sat back down in her chair and gazed at her darkened crystal ball.

"Let's get out of here," Ren whispered to Kip, grabbing hold of his arm and pulling him toward the exit.

"Why?" Kip asked.

"Because something's not right about this place," Ren said. "And that old woman in Room 1942, Mrs. Wellshire, told me to stay away from someone called the Tick-Tock Man. I didn't know what she meant, but that guy had a clock on top of his cane."

"You always think too much," Kip said.

"One of us has to," Ren replied.

Just as they were about to walk out of the tent, they heard Zora's voice whisper behind them, "Remember . . . nothing's free at the carnival. There's always a price."

Ren squinted at her, slightly disturbed. Her warning only enhanced the twisted feeling in his gut. Without saying anything back to Zora, he pulled Kip outside and checked his watch.

"You know, you don't have to look at your watch every five seconds," Kip said. "You'll miss the entire carnival."

Ren shrugged, as if to say, *Whatever*. "We still have an hour before Aunt Winnie is supposed to pick us up," he said. "We should wait outside the gates."

"But there are still a lot of rides we haven't ridden," Kip complained.

"I already told you—we're out of tickets," Ren said. "And this place gives me the creeps."

"You're such a scaredy-cat. The magician said there are other ways to pay for the rides," Kip replied.

"And you really want to stick around to find out what he means? Lesson number one in life: never trust a grown man wearing a cape," Ren said. "Let's go."

"If you want to wait outside, then go! But

I'm going to walk around some more until Aunt Winnie gets here."

"We need to stick together," Ren reminded him. "Like the girl said."

"I thought you didn't believe in all that hocus-pocus stuff."

"I don't," Ren replied, realizing that part of him did. "But I'm telling you, something's not right about this carnival."

Ren reached for Kip's arm, and Kip yelled, "Let go of me!"

A few carnival-goers stopped to examine the situation. Ren could feel their eyes poring over him.

"All right, I'm done," Ren said. "You want to walk around on your own, then go for it. I'm tired of being your babysitter. All I do is stand around being the responsible one while you get to have all the fun."

Ren turned his back on Kip and began to walk away.

"Fine!" he heard Kip shout.

Ren walked ten more yards, then looked

over his shoulder, expecting to see Kip still standing there.

But his little brother was already gone.

Ren shook his head and kept walking toward the gates. He made it another few steps before his conscience got the best of him and he felt his chest growing tighter.

What if something happens to Kip? he worried. *What if he gets hurt and I'm not there to help him? I can't just let him roam around the carnival on his own.*

Ren whirled around and scanned the crowd, looking for Kip's blue cap. But there were too many other people wearing similar hats.

He walked along the midway, examining the faces in each line, hoping to find his brother waiting to get on a ride. He heard frightened shrieks coming out of the Haunted Mirror Maze, terrified laughter echoing out of Clowntown, and blood-curdling screams pouring out from the Jaws of Death. But he didn't see Kip anywhere.

Ren sat down on a sarcophagus-shaped

bench and put his head in his hands.

If I don't find him soon, Aunt Winnie is going to kill me, he thought.

Right then, the chilly October breeze brushed over him.

Just as he was about to give up his search, he looked over and saw . . .

Kip.

Standing at the entrance to the Drop of Fear.

Talking to the man in the black cape.

8

REHEARSAL FOR DEATH

Ren sprinted toward them, but he was too late. The coffin lid closed, and Kip rose high in the sky on the rickety tracks.

"How did he get on? He didn't have any tickets left!" Ren shouted at the Tick-Tock Man.

"I told you, boy, there are other ways to pay the carnival," the magician said. "But fear not. Death comes to us all."

The strange man walked away, and Ren noticed the clock at the top of his cane was glowing. Even weirder, an eerie green mist was seeping out of it. Ren looked to see if the hands of the clock were turning backward, but he couldn't get a close enough view.

He then noticed other kids getting onto nearby rides without providing tickets. They simply walked to the front of the line, held out their right arm, showed a stamp or something to the carnie operator, and walked onto the ride. Ren wondered what they were using as payment.

His gaze turned up to Kip's coffin just as it came to a stop at the top of the track two hundred feet in the air. All the sounds around Ren disappeared as he held his breath, waiting for the coffin to drop. His stomach churned at the thought of being trapped in a box about to free-fall to the ground, and he wondered what Kip was feeling in that moment.

The costumed carnie operating the ride shouted a countdown into his giant megaphone. . . .

"Seven . . . Six . . . Five . . . Four . . . Three . . . Two . . . One . . ."

Then . . .

He pulled the lever.

The clicking sound of the tracks took Ren's breath away.

Whoosh!

Ren watched in breathless horror as the coffin fell, until it vanished into the dark gravelike cavity in the ground.

He ran past the ride operator and peered down at the coffin resting in the artificial grave.

"Hey, get back in line!" the carnie yelled at Ren. But Ren ignored him.

"Kip! Are you okay?" Ren called down to his brother, trying to pull open the lid. But it was locked tight.

He jerked at the lid again and again, hit it with his fists, pushed and pulled, but nothing worked.

The carnie operator laughed, which made Ren even more uncomfortable with the situation.

Finally, there was an angry hissing sound, like pressure being released beneath the ride.

Ren tried the handle again, and this time it opened.

But when he looked inside . . .

The coffin was empty.

Kip had vanished, just like the coin.

9

HAUNTED MIRROR MAZE

"It's impossible!" Ren said, examining the coffin, looking for any sign of Kip.

"You won't find him here," a familiar voice called out from behind Ren.

Zora stood next to the aggravated operator. She seemed to have appeared out of nowhere.

"Where is he?" Ren asked in a panic.

Zora walked over to the coffin and pressed a hidden button. A trapdoor at the bottom of the casket opened, and Ren observed a hole in the ground beneath it.

"All rides at the carnival are connected," she explained. "Like appendages of the same body.

This one leads to the Haunted Mirror Maze."

Ren looked down through the hole in the casket and realized that the entire carnival sat on some kind of platform.

"Your brother must have made a special transaction that allows him into the underground network of tunnels to skip the lines."

"Can you show me where he went?" Ren asked.

"I can try, but it may be too late."

"Too late for what?"

Zora didn't answer.

She took Ren's hand and led him through the crowd until they arrived at the entrance to the Haunted Mirror Maze. Spooky calliope music and sound effects echoed from within, seeping out into the crisp autumn night.

"I'll wait here," Zora said, handing Ren a ticket.

"You're not coming with me?" Ren asked.

"I don't do mirrors," Zora replied. "Kind of like how you aren't a fan of clowns."

"But . . . how could you even know that?" Ren asked.

"I saw it in my moon-ball," she said.

Ren looked into her eyes and realized she was serious.

Knowing he didn't have time to question her, he approached the ghostly entrance of the Haunted Mirror Maze. Fingers of fog curled out from a machine hidden somewhere inside.

He handed his ticket to a carnie, stepped into the swirling mist, and felt the world behind him slowly disappear.

"Kip! Are you in here? If you can hear me, say something!" Ren called out into the unknown.

Soon, mirrors and mist surrounded him in every direction. The walls, the ceiling, and the floor . . . were all his reflection, replicated dozens of times.

I can see why Zora was too creeped out to come in here, he thought.

But what he didn't know was that the creepiest part was still up ahead.

He turned down another hallway. And another.

Then, at the final turn, a foreboding voice filled his ears. . . .

"Joooiiinnn ussss, Ren."

It was deep and unnatural, like something out of a nightmare.

Ren spun around, stirring the fog, unable to tell if the voice was in his head or was coming from the mirrors.

"Hello?" he said.

But there was no reply.

Suddenly, Ren saw Kip's reflection pass over a single mirror, then quickly disappear.

"Kip!" Ren called out.

The mirror opened on its own, like a door into another world. Only blackness stared back at him.

Zora said all the rides are connected. Maybe this is the secret passageway to the next one, he thought.

Conjuring up his courage, Ren stepped through the doorway. The mirror-door shut behind him, trapping him alone in the darkness.

"H-hello?" he said again, then grew afraid that talking might draw attention to himself.

But there was only silence.

Maybe Zora wasn't really trying to help me. Maybe she was leading me into a trap, Ren thought.

He stepped farther into the unknown. And then took another step. And another. Until he saw a flickering light up ahead.

Another room, he thought, wondering if there was an end to the nightmarish labyrinth.

He approached the light and soon realized it was the flame of a candle. Cautiously, he picked up the antique candle-stand and started to turn in a circle.

But before he could make it all the way around, he stopped, paralyzed with fear.

Someone was standing in the shadows, watching him.

10

WHAT YOU SEE IS WHAT YOU GET

Ren stared back at the thing in the dark, waiting for it to move.

But it never did.

He held the candlelight closer to its face and saw that it wasn't a person at all. It was a life-size mannequin dressed like a clown. Its eyes seemed so real, like it was actually watching him, its gaze following him wherever he went.

The soft light revealed dozens of other mannequins and odd-shaped figures there too: porcelain dolls, broken ventriloquist dummies, stage props, and more.

It was a room filled with the creepiest things Ren had ever seen.

This must be where the carnies store all the stuff that they don't use anymore, he thought. *But why was there a candle lit unless someone else has been in here recently?*

He then noticed a broken mirror leaning up against a wooden chest full of dolls. It was grimy and covered in dust.

A warning had been painted over it in bloodred letters.

Beware.
This mirror is haunted.

Ren stepped toward the mirror and examined his own reflection.

But he didn't see himself staring back. . . .

He saw Kip.

"Help, Ren!" Kip's muffled voice cried out as he banged on the inside of the mirror.

"Kip! What's going on? How did you get in there?" Ren yelled.

He suddenly felt a void inside himself

widening, aching, making him hollow. He regretted all the times he had ever treated Kip badly and realized how much he wanted him to be okay.

But it was too late.

Kip's reflection soon faded.

Ren looked over every inch of the mirror, trying to re-conjure the image of his brother.

"Please come back, Kip! I'm sorry!"

Then Ren saw something floating toward him in the glass.

Something unnatural.

And ominous.

A black balloon, Ren thought. *When will this nightmare end?*

But it had only just begun.

Suddenly, the balloon popped. And a monstrous figure appeared in its place.

Its terrible, ugly grin smiled back at him. Yellow drool oozed from its decrepit mouth.

A bloodthirsty clown! Ren thought, trembling in terror.

The hideous monster stared back at him. With cocked fangs. And black eyes. But it didn't look like a human dressed as a clown. It looked more like a grotesque creature that had crawled out of the darkest dark.

Spookiest of all, when Ren moved his left arm, the clown moved its arm in exact synchronization. Their reflections were sewn together perfectly.

"Give me back my brother!" Ren yelled, summoning whatever courage he could find within himself.

But the clown only laughed.

Its laughter grew deeper and darker, until . . .

The hideous thing faded away.

And Ren was alone again.

He collapsed to the ground, as if the breath had been knocked out of him.

What was that . . . thing? he wondered, his hands still trembling.

Just as he was about to look for an exit, something caught his eye.

On the ground.

Right in front of the mirror.

Kip's blue cap.

11

GOOD NIGHT, SLEEP TIGHT

Ten minutes later, Ren was standing just inside the carnival gates talking to the sheriff on duty.

"I swear it, officer. There's something not right about this place. I saw my brother trapped inside a mirror with a clown monster, and—"

The sheriff began to laugh.

"Boy, I've heard some whoppers in my day, but this one takes the cake."

"Go see for yourself!" Ren pleaded.

Just then, the caped magician appeared, with Zora at his side. His elaborately ringed hand was on her shoulder, and she was looking at the ground, as if she was in trouble.

"Good evening, officer," the Tick-Tock Man said.

Ren couldn't believe he had the nerve to show his face after kidnapping Kip.

"That's him! That's the guy who took my brother," Ren said.

The magician smiled.

"Sheriff, it seems there's been some kind of misunderstanding," he said. "My daughter here was just playing a prank on the boy."

"Daughter?" Ren questioned him in surprise. "Prank?"

"Yes," the magician continued. "She thought it'd be funny to scare him in the Haunted Mirror Maze. She took his brother's cap while reading their fortunes and left it on the floor of the final room in the maze. A childish prank. But it's more than scared the boy. You see, the end of the maze is made to look like a secret room full of old abandoned props. The person looks into a mirror and sees their greatest fears. It's rigged, of course. But this boy here must have seen something about his brother."

Ren looked to Zora, wondering if it was true.

Even if it is true, how could they make something inside my head appear in a mirror? he thought.

"I know what I saw. And it wasn't just smoke and mirrors," Ren said.

The sheriff squinted at the magician, then at Ren, as if trying to decide who was telling the truth.

Finally, the sheriff burst into laughter again.

"This just keeps getting better. Haunted mirrors. Bloodthirsty clowns. Sounds like quite good entertainment for this time of year," he said, then turned to Ren. "Boy, why don't you go get some cotton candy and relax a bit? Carnivals are supposed to be fun."

"Because he's lying!" Ren said, beginning to feel helpless. "How can you just stand there and do nothing?"

Right then, Aunt Winnie pulled up in the black hearse.

The Sheriff, the Tick-Tock Man, and Zora watched with intrigue as the flustered woman jumped out of the funeral car and hurried toward Ren.

"What's going on here?" she asked.

"This guy is hiding Kip somewhere!" Ren said, pointing at the magician.

"What?" Aunt Winnie asked in shock. Ren was glad there was finally someone there who would believe him. "Kip is back at Old Manor, asleep. As soon as he showed up without you, I came right away. I told you two to stick together, but he said you left him. It's a good thing he found his way back on his own. What if something bad had happened to him?"

"Kip is asleep? In his bed at Old Manor?" Ren asked his aunt. "And he didn't look hurt or anything?"

"He just seemed tired. Didn't say much. Went straight to bed."

That doesn't sound like Kip, Ren thought. *He's never volunteered to go to bed on his own. His feelings must have been so hurt that he decided to walk home without me.*

Ren shot a questioning look at the magician, who raised his brows as if to say, *"See? I told you so."*

"I swear I saw him get on that ride, Aunt Winnie," Ren said. "And then I saw his reflection in the mirror and his hat and a clown and—"

The magician calmly handed Kip's cap to Aunt Winnie.

"I believe this belongs to your younger nephew, mademoiselle," he said charmingly, then took Aunt Winnie's hand and kissed the top of it.

She quickly pulled her hand back.

"Excuse me," she said, unimpressed by the stranger's charm.

The Tick-Tock Man glanced over at her hearse and said, "I'm sorry. I couldn't help but notice your . . . unique choice of transportation."

"It's a rental," Aunt Winnie replied.

"I see," the Tick-Tock Man said.

Not easily deterred, the magician flipped over his hand and conjured a black rose out of thin air.

"A beautiful flower for a beautiful lady," he

said, handing it to her.

She frowned at him suspiciously. For a moment, Ren thought she might reach for it, but she managed to resist.

"Thank you, but I don't care for roses—especially dead ones," she said, observing his wicked gray eyes.

There was an awkward pause, then the sheriff interrupted, "Well, I think our work here is done. I know boys sometimes get mixed up about what they see. No harm done as far as I can tell. Hope you folks have a spooky night."

The sheriff tipped his hat and walked back to his post.

The magician exchanged one last look with Ren, then turned and headed into the carnival crowds with Zora at his side.

She looked over her shoulder at Ren, and he saw some secret hiding in her eyes.

Aunt Winnie was quiet for most of the ride back to the nursing home. Ren could tell she was thinking about something. Just before she pulled into the parking lot of Old Manor, she said, "That man gave me a weird feeling. Stay away from him, okay?"

"You don't have to worry about that," Ren said. "I'm never going back there again."

As soon as Aunt Winnie parked the hearse, Ren went straight to his and Kip's room in the guest house. Sure enough, he found Kip fast asleep in his bed.

But what he didn't know was that the boy lying in the bed wasn't Kip. It wasn't a boy at all.

12

MORNING SICKNESS

When Ren walked into the kitchen for breakfast the next morning, Aunt Winnie was washing dishes in the sink.

"How did you sleep?" she asked.

"Okay, I guess," Ren replied.

"I have to go check on the residents, but you two are welcome to anything in the pantry or fridge for breakfast," she said. "Come on over to the main building when you're done. We have lots of decorating to do."

Before Ren could say anything, she disappeared out the door.

He took a bowl out of the pantry and sat down at the kitchen table to pour his cereal.

A few moments later, Kip walked in. His eyes looked glazed over, and he failed to acknowledge Ren's presence.

"That was some move walking home from the carnival on your own last night," Ren said. "I admit, you had me worried."

Kip didn't reply. He poured his cereal and began spooning it out of the bowl without adding milk.

Ren examined Kip's face and noticed that it was paler than usual. He didn't smile or laugh either, which wasn't like him. In fact, there hardly seemed to be any life in his eyes at all.

It was then that Ren noticed a swollen bite mark on Kip's right forearm.

"Dang. What bit you?"

But Kip kept staring at his bowl.

"Where did you go?" Ren asked. "After the Drop of Fear, I mean. You did get on the ride, didn't you?"

When Kip didn't answer for a third time, Ren raised his voice in frustration, "Are you sick or just ignoring me?"

Kip slowly looked up.

The skin around his eyes was dark, like he hadn't slept all night.

"You don't look so good," Ren said, getting the same pit in his stomach that he had the night before. "How did you pay for that ride last night? Did you make some special deal to skip the lines?"

Kip's flushed, crusty lips began to move, whispering something that Ren couldn't decipher. He kept repeating it over and over again. But it was too soft for Ren to hear.

Ren scooted closer and lowered his ear in front of Kip's mouth. . . .

"Beat, beat . . . Tick, tock . . . Every heart is a ticking clock."

Ren stood up, and his chair screeched across the floor. His stomach twisted into knots.

"W-why did you say that?" Ren asked.

Without giving an explanation, Kip rose from his chair.

"I'm tired," he said, walking to the kitchen

window and pulling down the blinds to block the sunlight. "I'm going back to bed."

Not knowing what to say, Ren watched as Kip walked across the kitchen toward the doorway.

But as Kip passed by the mirror on the wall, Ren's eyes widened in horror.

Kip was missing his reflection.

13

SECRET ON THE WALL

That's not possible, Ren thought, wondering what had happened to his brother's reflection.

He watched as Kip ambled down the hallway of the guest house and disappeared into his bedroom.

Maybe Mrs. Wellshire wasn't crazy after all. And maybe she knows what's going on, he thought.

Ren put his cereal bowl in the sink and headed out the kitchen door.

When he arrived at Mrs. Wellshire's room

in Old Manor a few minutes later, he heard her coughing. Each cough was followed by a painful wheeze.

The door was already slightly open, but he knocked on it anyway to announce his presence.

"Mrs. Wellshire? It's me—Ren. The boy who came by yesterday to check on you," he said, then stepped into her room.

She looked at him, then back to a book that was open in her lap. It was full of photographs, and Ren realized it was a scrapbook of some kind.

"Glad to see you survived the night," she said, turning to the next page. "It's my birthday, you know."

"I—I didn't know that," Ren replied, walking to her side. "Happy Birthday."

"Eighty-nine years old," she said. "Goes by in a blink. This book is all I have left of it. The memories, the adventures, the people. My husband passed a few years ago, and my kids all have their own lives and families. Even my grandkids are starting to have their own children now."

She pointed to the colorful hand-drawn cards taped to the wall.

"I receive one in the mail every week from my great-granddaughter."

Ren saw the pages of the scrapbook filled with black-and-white photos from long ago. Mrs. Wellshire no longer seemed like the ghoulish woman he had encountered the day before—her terror of the carnival seemed to have subsided. As she turned the pages, he saw glimpses from the story of her life. . . .

Her wedding day.

Her daughter's tenth birthday.

A Christmas morning with her kids.

She and her husband on a cruise ship.

"Life doesn't slow down for anyone," she said. "Best to enjoy it while you can."

Ren glanced down to check his watch but stopped himself.

"I came to ask you about the carnival," he said. "Something happened to my brother there last night. And this morning, he had a nasty bite on his arm, and—"

Before he could finish, Mrs. Wellshire turned

over her arm and pulled up her sleeve.

"Did it look like this?" she asked.

Ren examined her forearm, where a strange dark scar was striped across her withered flesh. The shape was the same as Kip's. It looked like a tiny bat.

"So whatever it was bit you too?" Ren asked.

"I warned you to stay far away from that place," Mrs. Wellshire said, pushing her sleeve back down.

"I didn't believe you," Ren confessed. "But I do now."

Mrs. Wellshire gazed at him for a moment, and Ren wondered what long-ago memories were reeling through her mind.

"What else can you tell me?" he asked.

The old woman leaned back in her chair and pointed to the wooden desk in the corner of the room.

"Look behind it," she said.

Curious, Ren walked over to the desk. He pulled it out toward him and noticed something carved onto the wall.

Herbert Copeland
Was Here

Ren squinted in confusion.

"Who's Herbert Copeland?" he asked.

"He lived in this room long before me. Died years ago, a few weeks after his one-hundred-and-first birthday. We were in kindergarten together just down the road from here. That boy had more freckles than you've ever seen."

Ren looked up at her.

"But . . . how's that possible? If he was one hundred and one when he died, he would have been a lot older than you. How could you two have been in kindergarten at the same time?"

Mrs. Wellshire took a deep breath through her nostrils and let it out slowly, as if she was debating whether to let Ren in on a secret.

Finally, she whispered mournfully, "It's because the carnival stole more from him than it did from me."

14

A TALE OF TWO SISTERS

"The carnival stole something from you?" Ren asked.

"Yes," Mrs. Wellshire said.

"I don't understand. Are you saying this same carnival came here when you were a kid?"

The old woman glanced to the doorway to make sure no one was eavesdropping. "It comes here once every seventy-seven years, when no one is left around to remember its last visit," she whispered. "But I remember. I remember it all."

Ren glanced out the window at the carnival

lights. He couldn't decide whether to trust Mrs. Wellshire.

"So what happened to my brother? Why is he different after riding the rides last night?"

"How did he pay?" Mrs. Wellshire asked.

"With tickets at first, then once we ran out . . . I don't know how he paid," Ren confessed.

Mrs. Wellshire sighed. "It was the same with my sister and me," she said.

"Your sister?"

"Yes. We were warned to stay away. But we snuck out that night anyway, unable to resist the carnival's alluring scents."

Ren knew exactly what she meant. Once exposed to the stimulating sights and smells, it was difficult to forget them.

"What happened?" he asked.

"After we ran out of tickets, a man wearing a black cape and with a clock on his cane told us we could give up a day of our lives to ride any ride our heart desired," Mrs. Wellshire said. "My sister and I both did it. Then afterward, he pointed to a much bigger, faster ride at the back of the carnival grounds and said we could give a month, or even a year, to ride that one. The faster the ride, the higher the price. And each ride . . . chose us. It all adds up quicker than most realize."

"You mean you paid with . . . time?"

"That's what it stole from us," Mrs. Wellshire said. "By the end of the night, I had already given up half a year of my life. I swore never to return. But my sister . . . she kept going back."

"How much time did she give up?"

"She couldn't get enough of the carnival's thrills, so on the final night she purchased the special ticket—the one with unlimited rides. I left after one night, but she stayed . . . forever."

Ren's head spun with questions. He couldn't believe what he was hearing.

"Do you think that's what my brother did?"

"From what you've told me, it doesn't sound like he's purchased the special ticket yet. But he's received the bite, and he'll try to go back again tonight."

"Is there any way to help him?"

Mrs. Wellshire opened her mouth to speak, but the urge to cough overcame her. She wheezed violently, and Ren wondered if he needed to go get help for her.

"I'm not sure," she said, clearing her throat. "But I know someone who might have the answers you need."

"Who?" Ren asked.

"My sister," Mrs. Wellshire whispered, then pulled out a gold necklace from beneath the neck of her gown. She clicked open the antique locket, revealing a small, faded black-and-white photograph inside. "Don't make the same mistake I did by letting the carnival take your brother. You have to find a way to stop him from going back tonight."

Ren's eyes widened in astonishment. The photo was unexplainable. In it were two girls about Ren's age. They both had dark hair and smiling eyes. And they looked identical. Just like . . .

"Zora," Ren whispered. "You were twins!"

15

LEAVE THE PAST IN THE PAST

It was only a couple miles to the carnival. The road outside the nursing home led straight to it. Ren ran some of the way, then walked, then ran again.

Along the path, he saw the same flyer stapled to every telephone pole he passed.

Don't Miss Halloween at the Carnival of Horrors!
Free rides until midnight for everyone who wears a mask!

When Ren finally arrived at the carnival gates, they were locked. He didn't see any carnies out on the midway, so he snuck through the bars of the entrance and went straight to Zora's tent.

The opening was tied off. Ren knelt down and raised the bottom of the canvas to peek inside. It was dark, and it didn't look like anyone was there.

"Hello? Zora?" he called out.

When no one answered, Ren glanced over his shoulder to see if anyone was watching, then he rolled under the flaps and into the tent. He heard a rustling behind a nearby drape, where he could see the corner of Zora's coffin-shaped bed.

That's why no one was on the midway, he realized. *Carnies must sleep during the day since they're operating the rides all night.*

"Who's there?" Zora finally called out.

"It's Ren. The boy you led into the Mirror Maze last night."

There was a moment of silence, then she replied, "Hold on. Just give me a second to put on my face."

He knew what she meant. His mom always said that when she didn't want anyone to see her without makeup.

A few moments later, Zora appeared in her full black attire.

"That was some prank you played on me last night—*if* it really was a prank," Ren said.

"I told you both to leave and never come back," she replied. "But you didn't listen."

"I came back because something happened to my brother," Ren continued. "I thought maybe you could tell me what's wrong with him."

"There's nothing you can do for your brother," Zora said. "He made his choice, and there's no turning back now. He's the only one who can stop himself."

She grabbed Ren's arm and pulled him toward the exit of the tent. Ren noticed that she was careful to stay in the shadows, untouched by sunlight.

Just before she threw him out, Ren shouted, "Your sister sent me!"

Zora stopped and peered at Ren. Stunned.

"You're lying. I don't have a sister," she said.

Ren reached into his pocket and pulled out Mrs. Wellshire's gold necklace. Zora's eyes grew wide.

"Impossible," she whispered. "Where did you get that?"

"Your sister loaned this to me so that you'd know she's still alive," Ren said.

Zora reached for a gold chain around her own neck and lifted an identical locket from beneath her shirt. She clicked it open, and a duplicate photo of Zora and Mrs. Wellshire as young girls stared back at Ren.

"I know all about how the carnival steals time from kids," Ren said. "I know that you should be really old, but you're somehow still young. And your sister—she wants you to come visit her."

Zora stuffed the locket back beneath her shirt.

"I can't. I wish I could, but that's not how things work here," she replied, then walked back across her tent and began setting up her table for the coming evening.

"Is it because of your father?" Ren asked.

Zora glanced up.

"The magician's not my real father," she explained. "He just took me in after I joined the carnival."

"Don't you at least want to send your sister a message? Something to tell her you haven't forgotten her?" Ren asked.

"No. I decided long ago that the past is best left in the past." Zora went back to organizing her table, then she paused and added, "How is she? My sister, I mean."

"She's had a good life, as far as I can tell," Ren said. "Had a family. Traveled a lot. She seems happy. But she's nearing the end."

"Having a family sounds nice," Zora whispered.

She set up tiny skulls and bewitching cards around the moon-ball.

Ren stepped toward her, sensing she was warming up to him.

"Can you please tell me how to fix my brother?" Ren asked.

"I'm sorry—it's too late. There are no refunds at the carnival," Zora revealed.

"What do you mean?"

She seemed to sense that Ren wasn't going to drop the subject, so she compromised. "Okay. I'll give you three questions. But then you have to promise to leave. Be aware. The magician can see and hear everything that goes on at the carnival."

16

THREE QUESTIONS

Ren thought hard. He wanted to use his questions wisely.

"Is the Tick-Tock Man the evil behind the carnival?" he asked.

"Yes and no," Zora revealed. "He's sort of like . . . its ambassador. He was just like you once. All of us were. But he's from a more ancient time. No one knows for sure how old he is."

Ren pondered her meaning, then moved on to his second question.

"Where did the carnival come from?"

Zora sat down at the table in front of her moon-ball. She looked at Ren as if she was afraid of what he might think if she told him the truth. "The carnival is . . . alive. It has existed since the beginning of time. Since the human heart was split into good and evil. The more deals the carnival made, the larger it grew. It preys upon the young, because they have the most currency to steal."

"Currency?" Ren asked. "You mean like . . . time?"

"Heartbeats," Zora corrected.

Ren suddenly remembered the bizarre words Kip had mumbled at the breakfast table: *"Beat, beat. Tick, tock. Every heart is a ticking clock."* Of course!

"Every person is born with a certain number of heartbeats—of ticks," Zora said. "The carnival feeds off them. It steals their seconds, minutes, hours, days, weeks, months, years, even decades. The customer decides in their heart what a ride is worth, and then they make payment. Giving up an hour of life for one ride is one thing. But two, three, four . . . quickly turn into twenty, thirty, forty. It becomes an addiction. And some, like your brother, can't get enough. They keep coming back. And eventually pay the ultimate price."

"His life?" Ren asked.

Zora shook her head.

"A life can come and go, but there's only one thing that lasts forever: the soul," Zora said. "For unlimited rides, the customer has to be willing to sell it. Because of the bite, the Tick-Tock Man already has your brother's soul in his possession, though it hasn't been cashed in yet. But if your brother chooses to make the final transaction on Halloween night, he'll be bound to the carnival until the end of time."

Ren couldn't believe what he was hearing. Kip was on the verge of selling his soul so that he would never have to grow up and could ride the carnival's rides forever.

"You've already used up your three questions," Zora said. "But I'll give you one more."

It was too hard to pick just one. But Ren

decided there was one that was more important than all the others.

"How can I get back the heartbeats that Kip already sold?"

"I told you, there are no refunds," Zora said.

Ren sighed, feeling defeated.

"There is one way you could possibly trick the carnival. But it's forbidden," Zora said.

"What is it?" Ren pleaded.

Before Zora could reply, she looked up at something behind Ren and instantly grew paralyzed. Ren was just about to turn around to see what she was looking at when . . .

A black bag was thrown over his head. Something pounded against his skull. And all went dark.

17

CARRIAGE OF SOULS

When he woke up some time later, all he heard was the sound of ticking. Ren wasn't sure where he was. It was too dark to see anything. He suspected he must still be somewhere at the carnival, because he heard screams and laughter nearby.

But when he shouted for help, the rides were too loud for anyone to hear him.

Ren groped around in the dark and discovered what felt like a small barred window. He opened the blackened pane, and dusty moonlight poured in, casting a soft light in his prison cell.

He was in a carriage of some kind.

And the walls were full of . . .

Clocks.

Hundreds of them. Each one hung on a nail or sat on a shelf. Ticking, tocking, ticking, tocking.

Strangest of all, there was a wooden coffin on the floor nearby, with red satin sheets spilling out of it.

What's that doing here? Ren thought. *Is someone planning to bury me in it?*

An unfamiliar voice drifted out of the darkness. "Welcome to the Carriage of Souls."

Ren froze, realizing he was not alone. He saw someone crouching in the corner of the room inside another cage.

He squinted, trying to get a better look.

But his eyes soon widened in horror.

The mysterious figure was wearing a tattered tuxedo and was sitting with his back against the wall. His head was twice the size of a normal human head and didn't have a single wisp of hair.

Instead, it had . . .

Orange flesh.

A green stem.

And a set of eyes, a nose, and a jagged mouth cut out like a jack-o'-lantern's.

Ren scooted back against the wall in fright.

Johnny Pumpkinhead, he thought, remembering the painting of him on the side of the freak show tent. *I thought he was just a gimmick, but . . . he looks so real.*

"What do you want?" Ren asked.

The jack-o'-lantern face suddenly blazed to life, emitting a saffron glow.

"Many things," the stranger replied.

"W-where am I? Why are we here?" Ren asked, terrified at the sight of the impossible creature before him.

Johnny Pumpkinhead laughed.

"Indeed. 'Where are we? Why are we here?' Perhaps the two oldest human questions," Johnny Pumpkinhead said, swatting at several flies buzzing around his rotted head.

"Who put us here?" Ren asked.

"The Tick-Tock Man, of course," Johnny Pumpkinhead replied.

Ren thought about it for a moment, then nodded toward the coffin.

"Is he planning to kill us?"

Johnny Pumpkinhead spit out a pumpkin seed and shook his head.

"That's where he sleeps. It's his bed," he explained.

A shiver ran up Ren's spine.

"Are all the carnies . . . dead?" he asked.

"On the contrary. We're all very much alive. *Very* much," Johnny Pumpkinhead replied.

Ren gazed around the room, and the sound of ticking grew louder in his ears.

"And the clocks? Why are there so many of them?" he asked.

Johnny Pumpkinhead pulled himself up by the bars of his cage and stood the best he could.

"They aren't just clocks," he answered.

"What are they, then?"

"Souls," Johnny Pumpkinhead revealed,

and the buttery light within his head grew dimmer.

"Souls?" Ren asked.

"Yes. As soon as a customer receives the bite, their soul-clock appears here in the Tick-Tock Man's carriage. Until the Feast of Souls on Hallows' Eve."

"What happens then?"

"Do you really want to know? It's quite terrible," Johnny Pumpkinhead warned.

Ren glanced around at all the clocks, wondering which one belonged to Kip. It was impossible to tell. All he wanted to do was find Kip's clock.

"Is there a way out of here?" Ren asked.

"Depends. Have you received the bite yet?" Johnny Pumpkinhead inquired, though Ren had the feeling that the stranger somehow already knew the answer.

"No," Ren replied.

"Then there might still be a way for you to escape. But there's no use in running—you'll ask for the bite sooner or later. They always do," Johnny Pumpkinhead said, then spit out another seed.

He pointed to the coffin, and Ren remembered the trap door that had been in the bottom of the one on the ride.

"It's a trick coffin," Johnny Pumpkinhead began. "The Tick-Tock Man uses it onstage for his final disappearing act. The bottom falls out, leading to an otherworldly realm—or perhaps simply to a secret exit beneath the carriage. Like it did for your brother on the Drop of Fear."

"But what about the lock on these bars?" Ren asked, distracted by his current predicament.

Johnny Pumpkinhead reached into his pocket and pulled out a small item. He scooted closer to Ren's cage, put his jack-o'-lantern face near the bars, and offered the tiny object to him.

"Take this. It's one of Scary Mary's hairpins. You can use it to pick the lock."

Ren began to reach for it but stopped himself. Something Johnny Pumpkinhead had said bothered him.

"H-how did you know my brother went

through the bottom of a trick coffin? I never said anything about that," Ren said.

Johnny Pumpkinhead laughed.

"It's been the word on the street, that's all," he replied.

Ren decided it was possible that other carnies knew what had happened the night before.

"What did you say you're in here for?" Ren asked.

"Does it really matter?" Johnny Pumpkinhead said.

Ren knew he didn't have enough time to wait around for an answer, so he went ahead and reached for the hairpin.

But when his hand touched Johnny Pumpkinhead's fingers, something awful happened. . . .

The fantastical creature's tough orange skin began to melt, the light of his eyes snuffed out, and his pumpkin head spun upon his neck like a basketball.

Soon, his entire body morphed into something else.

Into someone else.

The Tick-Tock Man! Ren thought in horror. *Johnny Pumpkinhead was only a disguise!*

The bars of the cage vanished, and the Tick-Tock Man gripped Ren's arms like vises.

The magician lifted Ren into the air with superhuman strength and laughed like a madman.

"Let me go!" Ren shouted, his legs dangling.

"Not until you swear to keep everything you know a secret!"

"I—I swear!" Ren said.

The Tick-Tock Man squeezed tighter.

"Don't lie to me, boy. I know what you're up to. And if you keep going down that path, it won't end well."

The Tick-Tock Man opened his mouth, and a green fog drifted out of his throat toward Ren.

Just before Ren breathed it in, he kicked the magician in the stomach.

The Tick-Tock Man lurched over, dropping Ren. The frightened boy leaped toward the wooden coffin at the center of the carriage, activated the secret door, and jumped in.

"Your brother will never escape! Never!" the Tick-Tock Man shouted after him.

As Ren descended through the bottom of the carriage, the ticking of the soul-clocks and the shouts of the magician grew farther and farther away.

He crawled out from beneath the carriage and sprinted away from it as fast as he could.

When he glanced back over his shoulder, he saw one word painted across the side of the carriage in giant red letters:

CARNEVIL

18

BANISHMENT

The carnival was alive. The smells, the sounds, the sights . . . were all ablaze.

It's already late! I have to get back to Old Manor to stop Kip from coming here, Ren thought.

As Ren made his way through the crowd, he felt the rides pulling at him like magnets. He couldn't explain it, but it was much harder to resist them than it had been the night before. As soon as he found the strength to walk away from one of them, another lured him in. He felt like a puppet being tugged by a dozen different strings. And each time, he had to find the strength to cut the string that pulled at him the hardest.

For what seemed like hours, he was a mouse trapped in a maze, unable to find his way out. He craved the brain-fried funnel cakes, the bloodstained cotton candy, the liver-flavored lemonade, and he became more and more curious about the dark wonders behind each ride's door.

Just when he thought he could no longer resist the temptations of the carnival, he saw . . .

Kip.

Looking a bit older than he had that morning.

And his darkened eyes were full of craving.

He's already here! Ren thought.

Kip skipped the line at Clowntown and ran straight through the ride's entrance.

No! Ren thought. *I have to get him out of here!*

Too afraid to go inside Clowntown, Ren waited outside for Kip to return.

A few minutes later, he saw Kip appear

across the jack-o'-lantern-lit midway on the Skeleton Coaster, looking older than a few moments before.

Ren tried to catch up to him, but Kip disappeared onto another ride.

And another.

And another.

Until Ren finally gave up.

Every time he gets on a ride, he comes off looking taller and older, Ren thought. *It's like the rides are fast-forwarding his aging process. I have to find a way to get his soul-clock back before it gets any worse.*

Knowing he couldn't help Kip if he was tempted by the carnival any longer, he crept behind a tent where there were no crowds, trying to make his way through the maze of jack-o'-lanterns to the carnival gates.

But soon, he heard two voices arguing nearby. . . .

"What you did is forbidden," a familiar voice said. "Taking the heart of the carnival out of safekeeping could ruin everything. If it ever traveled beyond the boundary, it could destroy the backward clock."

"I only wanted to see the heart up close," the other voice returned.

Ren glanced around the corner of the tent and saw the Tick-Tock Man scolding a carnie at the edge of the carnival grounds. In secret.

"If you can't obey the laws of the carnival, then maybe you no longer deserve its gifts," the magician threatened.

The carnie's eyes grew wide, as if he knew that beneath the magician's words was a dire threat. He looked at the Tick-Tock Man in terror.

"I swear I won't ever go near it again. Just please let me stay," the carnie pleaded.

"I'm afraid it's too late for that. You were told when you joined us that I have a no-tolerance policy on this issue."

The Tick-Tock Man took a step toward him.

The carnie opened his mouth to plead for mercy. But before a single word could escape his lips, the magician pushed him beyond the carnival boundary.

The carnie screamed.

As soon as his feet touched the ground beyond it, his body began to wither.

At first, Ren thought his eyes were playing tricks on him. But within seconds, the carnie turned into an old man, then into a decrepit corpse with hollowed eyes and yellowed flesh, then his corpse crumbled to dust and blew away in the October wind.

19

MONSTER IN THE HOUSE

R en couldn't believe his eyes.

The carnie was gone. Forever.

Carnies can't step beyond the boundary of the carnival, Ren realized. *That's why Zora said she couldn't leave to visit her sister.*

The Tick-Tock Man glanced in Ren's direction, and Ren quickly hid behind a tent. He waited until he saw the Tick-Tock Man's shadow disappear around the corner.

A few moments later, Ren sprinted through the carnival gates and back into the quiet world beyond.

The two miles back to Old Manor seemed like an eternity.

Coyotes howled from the forest.

Creatures lurked in the fields.

And hungry eyes stared back at him from the wild darkness.

Even the flyers stapled to the telephone poles seemed to glow in the dark, possessed by some strange magic that Ren had never known existed.

All the while, he thought of ways he might be able to trick the magician into getting close enough to the boundary to push him beyond it. Then perhaps all the deals would be voided—including Kip's.

When he arrived back at Old Manor, he found Aunt Winnie helping the residents carve pumpkins for the jack-o'-lantern contest in the main hall.

"Hi, Ren. How was the carnival?" she asked.

"It's evil!" Ren shouted. "It takes kids' souls and makes them grow up overnight!"

"What are you talking about?" she said,

putting down her carving knife and walking toward him, a concerned look in her eyes. "How many funnel cakes did you eat tonight?"

"You have to listen to me, Aunt Winnie," Ren replied. "The magician—he's—"

"I thought I told you to stay away from that man," Aunt Winnie said.

Before Ren could explain, he heard the front door of Old Manor open. A teenage boy walked inside. The stranger looked about seventeen years old and seemed to know his way around. He walked into the next room, sat down in a chair, and stared out the window toward the carnival, his gaze unmoving, as if lost in a trance.

That's when Ren realized . . .

The stranger was wearing Kip's blue cap.

Kip? Ren thought, suddenly recognizing the young man's eyes. *He's already aged ten years!*

"Look, Aunt Winnie! Kip looks like a teen-ager now!" Ren said.

"What in the world, Ren?" Aunt Winnie asked in surprise, not understanding why he would say such a thing. She glanced at Kip in the other room, then back to Ren. "Kip still looks nine and not a day older. By the way, I left some homemade cookies in the kitchen at the guest house. Why don't you take your brother over to eat a few and watch one of those monster marathons?"

Ren glanced over at Kip, then back to Winnie.

"You mean . . . you don't see it?"

"See what?" Aunt Winnie asked.

When Ren turned back to Kip, he was gone.

The front door was open, and Kip was walking back toward the guest house.

"Never mind," Ren said to Winnie, then hurried after his brother.

Aunt Winnie squinted, confused. She watched Ren as he ran out the door toward the guest house.

Once inside, Ren smelled the pumpkin–chocolate chip cookies that Aunt Winnie had made for them. He was tempted to take a bite, but his concern for Kip far outweighed his hunger.

As he walked down the hallway toward their room, he heard Kip talking to someone. . . .

"What if my aunt gets suspicious?" Kip asked.

It was the magician's voice that returned. "Her eyes won't see the truth until after the carnival leaves town at midnight on Hallows' Eve. No need to wait until tomorrow night. You can join us now, Kip. But I can only come to the other side if you invite me."

The Tick-Tock Man is in our room! Ren thought in horror. *But—how did he cross the carnival boundary?*

Ren cracked open the door and saw Kip sitting before the vanity mirror in the dark. There was no reflection in the glass, and no one else in the room.

Where is the voice coming from? Ren wondered, perusing the room for any sign of the magician. Then the truth hit him . . . *the mirror!*

The glass began to glow eerie green like a witch's cauldron.

Kip reached his hand toward the mirror,

until his fingers melted through into the swirling portal of twisted magic.

"No!" Ren shouted.

He ran into the room and tackled his brother away from the bewitched mirror. Kip's chair fell over, and the green glow of the glass extinguished.

All was dark and silent.

"I'm tired," Kip muttered, as if nothing out of the ordinary had just taken place.

He stood, took off his shoes, and climbed into the bottom bunk of the bed with his clothes still on. Ren realized that Kip's shirt, pants, and shoes had somehow grown along with his body. It was all part of the aging illusion.

Ren looked at his brother, not knowing what to do.

He then peered out the window at the silhouetted tombstones of the graveyard.

A moment later, Ren saw a lone bat fly across the pale October moon.

Sleeps in a coffin during the daytime.

Doesn't have a reflection.

He can only enter a house when he's invited.

Ren's eyes widened in horror.

The Tick-Tock Man is a . . . vampire? But that's impossible!

20
PREPARATIONS

The next day was Halloween.

Kip slept all morning while Ren ran around the nearby neighborhoods handing out flyers that he had made to try to lure kids away from the carnival.

They read:

> *Come to the Creepiest Place in Town*
> *This Halloween . . .*
> *Old Manor Nursing Home!*
> *A Haunted Hearse, Scary Stories, and*
> *Lots of Candy!*

By early afternoon, the sky was filled with dark clouds. But they didn't seem to move. They just sat there, as if waiting for the autumn wind to tell them where to go.

Ren spent the afternoon hanging garlic on every door of Old Manor so that the vampire-carnies couldn't get in. Then he put on his skeleton costume. It was a black long-sleeve shirt and pants with white bones painted over them. Aunt Winnie had bought him a skeleton mask at the local costume store to go with it. He then helped dress the residents in their costumes and makeup. Most of them said they hadn't had so much fun since they were kids.

Nearby, Aunt Winnie practiced her witch's cackle while she helped Kip put on his mummy costume, not noticing that he no longer looked like a boy. She was surprised when she ran out of gauze from the medicine cabinet.

I have to find a way to get Kip's soul-clock back before midnight, Ren thought, more worried than ever about his little brother. *As soon as the carnival opens, I'll sneak in to find it in the magician's carriage.*

After Aunt Winnie finished mummifying Kip, Ren approached her.

"Aunt Winnie, no matter what happens tonight, we can't let Kip leave Old Manor. He has to stay as far away from the carnival as possible, okay?" Ren warned her, then removed his skeleton mask.

"Ren, I already told you I'd help watch Kip so you can have fun tonight. And I admit, that place is weird, but it's just a dime-a-dozen Halloween carnival, that's all. Your imagination is getting the best of you. As long as you stay away from that man in the cape, you'll be fine."

Ren put his hands on her arms and stared into her eyes.

"Listen, if you ever do anything for me in my entire life, please do this one thing," Ren pleaded, his eyes as solemn as twin graves.

Aunt Winnie squinted, concerned.

"Okay, Ren," she replied, rebalancing her black witch's hat atop her head. "I won't let Kip leave Old Manor tonight. But only if you go down to the basement and bring up that last box of decorations." Aunt Winnie winked.

"No problem," Ren said, breathing a sigh of relief.

"Here, take this," Aunt Winnie added, grabbing a flashlight from the nearby table and handing it to Ren. "I already cut off the electricity in the basement to give it an eerie ambience for when the trick-or-treaters go down to the Morbid Mortuary scene tonight."

Ren smiled, took the flashlight, then headed down the hallway toward the basement door.

Where a shocking secret had been hidden for seventy-seven years.

21

BASEMENT SECRETS

The door to the basement was covered in black butcher paper with spooky words written on it.

Morbid Mortuary!

When Ren pushed open the door, it screeched like a cat being stepped on.

Only darkness stared back at him.

He turned on the flashlight, and the dusty beam of light licked the dark walls. Each step creaked beneath his feet as he crept down the stairs to the dungeon below.

Thunder rumbled outside, conjuring goose bumps on his skin.

Once his tennis shoes touched the concrete floor, he stepped carefully through the maze of cobwebbed mannequins and wax figurines all around him.

He passed by the mortuary table in the center of the room, where a bloodstained sheet covered a fake corpse. Bloody tubes ran out of the veins of the cadaver. And even though Ren knew it was fake and that Aunt Winnie had set it up the day before, his heart still thumped in his chest.

His flashlight beam moved over the room until it finally illumined the sealed box of decorations. He quickly grabbed it and was about to head back up the stairs when something else caught his eye.

In the farthest corner of the basement was a veil of cobwebs hiding something ancient.

He cautiously approached it, then peeled away the tangled webs until he could make out what lay beneath.

What is this doing down here? he wondered, running his hand over an antique file cabinet.

He squatted to open the drawers and discovered hundreds of dusty files within it.

"This must be where they used to store the records of Old Manor," he whispered.

He perused the files and realized they were sorted by years.

I wonder if . . . , he thought, thumbing through the files.

He stopped when he saw a section of files labeled "Unknown Identities." It was different from the other files in that it was marked with both red and black ink.

He pulled it out of the drawer and examined the folder.

Each file contained a paper-clipped photograph of an old person. There were at least a dozen of them, and they were all labeled "John Doe" or "Jane Doe." Ren knew those were generic names detectives used on mystery shows when they didn't know the actual identity of a person. But the strangest thing of all was that every single one of them had been checked in to the nursing home on the first day of November.

That's weird, he thought. *All these old people showed up at Old Manor the day after Halloween . . . exactly seventy-seven years ago.*

Behind the files was a yellowed newspaper clipping. It read:

Parents Report Missing Children after Carnival Leaves Town.

Meanwhile, Record Number of Elderly Check In to Local Nursing Facility

Claiming the Identities of the Missing Children

Ren felt a shiver down his spine. According to what he was reading, everything that Mrs. Wellshire had told him was true.

After the carnival left town, people could finally see the kids as their aged selves. But no one recognized them, so they couldn't go back home, Ren realized. *And that's what will happen again tomorrow morning if I don't find a way to defeat the carnival.*

Ren knew it was up to him to save Kip and all the infected kids in town.

He then noticed a file with a photo of a bald man with sunken eyes and countless faded freckles on his withered skin. The message typed beneath it read:

Name: John Doe
Claims to be missing local child Herbert Copeland
Estimated Age: 101

That's the man who carved his name on the wall in Mrs. Wellshire's room, Ren realized. *He didn't die just a few years ago—he died seventy-seven years ago! If I don't do something, dozens of new John Does and Jane Does are going to be checking in to Old Manor tomorrow, claiming to be missing kids.*

He knew there was only one person who could help him. One person who had been around for it all the last time the carnival had come to town. And still remembered.

* * *

When Ren arrived at Mrs. Wellshire's room, a jack-o'-lantern flickered on her windowsill while she slept in her bed. Her back was to the door, so he quietly approached her.

"Mrs. Wellshire?"

She didn't answer.

He touched her arm to see if she was okay, and it felt cold as ice.

Then, like a scary scene in a movie, the old woman turned over and hissed at him.

And that's when Ren saw her vampire fangs, dripping with blood.

22

CHECKMATE

Mrs. Wellshire reached for Ren's throat, and he stumbled backward onto her couch. His heart felt like it was about to explode in his chest.

She's one of them! Ren thought.

And then he fainted.

Moments later, he woke up in the dark, his vision blurry.

He saw Mrs. Wellshire's silhouette sitting up in her bed across from him.

Afraid, Ren jolted back, wondering if she had already bitten him.

Just as he was about to check his forearm, he saw her bloodied fangs sitting on the tray table beside her bed.

"Are you okay, boy? I didn't mean to scare you so bad," she said. "They were going around giving out Halloween props, and I took the fanged dentures. Thought it might be fun to give you a good fright tonight."

"I thought you were a—a . . . ," Ren started, unable to finish.

"There, there. I may be scary, but it's only because I'm old," she said with a laugh.

He wondered if she knew what the carnies really were. But he didn't want to upset her.

"Are you going to dress up for the Haunted Manor like all the other residents?" Ren asked, sitting up on the couch.

"Ha! I spend every breath trying to stay out of the Land of the Dead and then your aunt decides to bring it here," she joked. "Halloween is fun for kids, but for folks like me who are two steps away from the grave . . . it can be all too real."

She pointed out the window to the foggy graveyard. Hundreds of tombstones were silhouetted against the stormy-green sky. The carnival lights glowed beyond it.

Mrs. Wellshire coughed into her hands.

"Can I get you anything?" Ren asked.

"Just pull up a chair and keep an old woman company. Do you play chess?"

"I've played with my dad a few times," Ren said, and she pointed to the chessboard in the corner.

"My sister and I used to play all the time."

Ren dragged a chair beside her bed and set up the chessboard on the food table. But all he could think about was what he had found down in the basement.

"Mrs. Wellshire, do you remember when all the old people were moved into the Manor after the carnival left town seventy-seven years ago?"

"Oh yes," she replied, moving up one of her pawns. "There were endless rumors flying around town. And the missing kids—and the old people claiming to be the kids—it's all we talked about at school."

"Did you ever try to tell anyone about what happened to your sister?" Ren asked.

"I tried to tell a lot of people—my teachers, my neighbors—but no one believed me. Eventually, it seemed like everyone had forgotten her. I spent half my youth in the town museum, researching the past visits of the carnival. But I always ran into dead ends. It's as if the carnival erased any trace of itself—and the kids it took— from the town's memory."

"So it's true that grown-ups can't see the kids' actual ages until after the carnival leaves town?"

"If you're talking about that young man in the hallway, I know he's your little brother," she said, pointing to the seventeen-year-old Kip who was walking down the hallway in his costume, dragging one gauze-covered leg behind him like a mummy. "Your aunt won't see it until after the carnival leaves town. *If* there are any aged kids who are left behind this time. But any of us who have received a bite have eyes to see the darkness at any time."

"So will others like him show up tomorrow morning after the carnival leaves?"

"Only the few souls who find the strength to walk away from the carnival after they've received the bite. I was one of them. And so far, you've been strong enough to resist the bite altogether. Maybe it's because we were both thinking more about our siblings than our-selves. But even for the lucky ones who escape, their lives will never be the same. Whatever life they have left will always be haunted. Most have already given up too many heartbeats to fully be themselves again."

Ren handed her the locket she had loaned to him. She took it into her hands and gazed upon the photograph.

"I should have kept fighting for my sister when I was your age. I shouldn't have just given up. Maybe things would have turned out differ-ent."

Ren thought of Kip and didn't want to have the same regrets as Mrs. Wellshire.

He moved up one of his bishops on the chessboard. "I heard the Tick-Tock Man talking to a carnie last night. They said something about breaking the backward clock by taking the heart of the carnival beyond the boundary. I guess what I'm asking is . . . do you think the carnival can be destroyed? Like, for good?"

She thought for a moment, and Ren could tell she had considered the question before.

"I suppose if you found a way to stop feeding it, you could starve it for a while," she replied. "If the kids stopped riding its rides, eating its food, coveting its thrills, then I suppose the carnival would eventually die. Or at least move on to some other place."

Ren thought of the black cats roaming around the carnival grounds, then said, "Like a stray cat that stops getting scraps from one house and so moves on to another?"

"Exactly," Mrs. Wellshire said. "But it won't be that easy. It never is. I'm sure you wouldn't be the first to try."

"If I go back, I'm afraid I won't be able to

resist it anymore. It nearly brainwashed me last night. I wish I knew a way not just to starve it so that it will leave but to defeat it once and for all. Tonight. Forever. So that it can never steal another soul again."

Mrs. Wellshire made her next move on the chessboard.

"Checkmate," she said.

Ren looked down in surprise and realized he had missed a play.

Mrs. Wellshire smiled. "You know, my sister always used to say that you have to think two steps ahead of your opponent and not let them know your next move. Then you have to strike their heart as quickly as possible."

Ren's eyes grew wide.

The heart of the carnival, he thought.

"Every conscious thing has a heart," Mrs. Wellshire continued, as if trying to give Ren a clue.

"So . . . if the carnival is alive, then where is its heart?" he asked.

Mrs. Wellshire looked out the window to

the neon lights and big tops in the near distance. The black Ferris wheel with purple lights seemed to be smiling back at them as dozens of adult-size trick-or-treaters swarmed toward the carnival grounds.

"The Ferris wheel?" Ren said.

"Perhaps," Mrs. Wellshire replied. "After all, everything is built around it, protecting it like a a fortress or a rib cage."

Just then, the grandfather clock in the corner of her room rang nine times.

"You'd better hurry, boy," Mrs. Wellshire said. "The Tick-Tock Man will collect the final payment at midnight. And all transactions will be final."

23

OUTSMARTING THE WHEEL

Before he left Old Manor, Ren locked Kip inside their windowless room with enough food and water to last until he returned. Kip fought him like a rabid animal, but Ren fought harder. Then Ren hid the key so that there was no chance of Kip escaping, or of anyone letting him out. He even told Aunt Winnie he had decided to let Kip go trick-or-treating with him so she wouldn't get worried and go looking for Kip.

When Ren stepped outside, lightning flashed, and a loud grumble of thunder followed a few moments later.

He hurried down the main road toward the carnival grounds, running past dozens of masked trick-or-treaters who were on their way to another night of thrills.

"Stay away from the carnival! Go back home!" Ren shouted at them.

But no one heeded his warning.

He overheard one girl dressed as a princess chatting away to her friend dressed like a robot, "It was so weird. My sister looks like she's twenty now, but Dad still thinks she looks like she's ten."

Kids all over town must be experiencing the same thing, Ren thought. *After tomorrow, either the kids who have been bitten will leave with the carnival and their loved ones will eventually forget about them—or the aged kids will look too old for anyone to recognize them.*

It wasn't until Ren arrived at the bat-shaped gates and peered out onto the midway that he realized that many of the trick-or-treaters were under some evil spell. Not only that, but they didn't look like normal kids. Their costumes were kidlike, but the people beneath them were much older. Some looked like teenagers, others like middle-aged adults, and Ren even saw the withered skin of old people beneath several of the costumes.

These all must be the kids who were bitten, gave up heartbeats, and have aged at an astronomical rate, Ren thought.

While sneaking toward the Carriage of Souls, Ren passed by Zora's lantern-lit tent. She was inside reading the fortunes of two new customers who were both wearing pirate costumes. His instincts told him to go on, but there was something he wanted to ask her.

As soon as the two customers left her tent, Ren snuck inside.

When Zora saw him, she stood from her chair.

"What are you doing here?" she asked.

"You knew he could hear us last night when you told me I could ask three questions. Why did you let him take me?" Ren asked.

"I was protecting you," she replied.

"From what?"

"I warned you that he can hear everything if

he wants to. If I had tried to help you, he would have killed us both," she explained. "It was better for me to keep his confidence."

Ren wasn't sure he could trust Zora's words.

"It doesn't matter now," he said. "I need your help."

"With what?" she asked.

"I need to steal back my brother's clock before it's fed to the carnival tonight," Ren said. "Can you tell me how to get into the Carriage of Souls without being caught?"

Zora shook her head. "Even if you were able to recover your brother's soul-clock, you wouldn't be able to get back the time that's already been stolen from him. You might be able to save the heartbeats that remain, but if he chooses to feed his soul-clock to the carnival, there's no turning back."

"I made sure Kip won't have a chance to choose," Ren said.

"Don't be so sure," Zora warned. "The magician always finds a way to get what he wants. Besides, anything that belongs to the carnival that travels beyond its boundary will cease to exist. Including your brother's soul-clock. You'd have to destroy the carnival first."

"That's exactly what I plan to do," Ren said. "Once I can get close enough to the heart of the carnival."

Zora's eyes widened, as if she was surprised he knew about such a thing.

"The magician will never let you near it," she said.

"I'll find a way," Ren replied. "I have one question, though. If I destroy the carnival's heart, what will happen to you?"

Zora didn't answer, but Ren sensed the truth in her eyes.

"Come help me," he said. "I know that you regret giving your soul to this place. But there's still time for you to make things right."

Zora shook her head.

"Whatever good that was in me died a long time ago," Zora said.

"But what you're doing here—it's not natural; it's not right," Ren replied. "The wheel of life is supposed to move forward, not backward.

We all owe a death for a life. And to never pay what we owe is sort of like . . . stealing."

"Or just outsmarting the wheel," Zora replied. There was silence for a moment, then she continued, her emotions escalating. "You think you're the first person who's tried to convince me to turn against the carnival? What's done is done. There's no going back now. No changing sides."

"But that's not true. There are two sides to every coin, remember?" Ren said, pointing to the gold coin on her table. "There's always time to change. Otherwise, what's the point?"

He noticed Zora's eyes were misty, and he sensed that there was a great battle taking place within her.

"Please leave now. I have a big night ahead," she said, pushing Ren out of the entrance of her tent. She closed the flaps behind him and tied them off so that he couldn't come back inside.

Disappointed, Ren turned and crept along the jack-o'-lantern–lit midway, staying in the shadows as best he could. The grinning pumpkins blazed with an eerie light, as if they knew some dark magic was approaching.

When Ren arrived at the Carriage of Souls, the door was locked, just as he suspected it would be.

A cold wind blew over him.

Unsure what to do next, he put his hands in his pockets to keep them warm, and his fingers touched something cold.

He pulled a mysterious relic from his pocket and peered down at it.

A skeleton key, he thought. *It looks a hundred years old. Zora must have put it in my pocket when she pushed me out of her tent.*

Grateful, Ren inserted the key into the lock and turned it. Then he pushed open the door and cautiously stepped inside. He looked around for Kip's soul-clock and hoped to save as many others as he could.

But when the moonlight spilled into the carriage, Ren saw that all the clocks were gone.

24

FEAST OF SOULS

Dread rushed over Ren.

How can I save Kip if I can't find his clock? he wondered in desperation, noticing that the coffin was missing too. *I can't give up. I have to find a way.*

Just then, a purple mist reached into the carriage and grabbed hold of his nostrils. It was the same scent he had smelled when he stepped off the train three days before—the delicious, irresistible temptation that was the carnival.

Somewhere in the distance, calliope music played like a funeral song. It lured him back outside, where a crowd of spellbound trick-or-treaters swarmed toward the dark heart of the carnival. They each wore a different mask and carried a blazing jack-o'-lantern in their hands.

Pretending to be under the same spell, Ren pulled on his skeleton mask, joined the Halloween masquerade, and followed the music, resisting the pull of each ride along the way.

When he arrived at the center of the grounds, he saw a giant performance stage in front of a dozen wooden church pews, where all the trick-or-treaters began to sit down. The stage was framed by massive black curtains that reached so high into the sky, Ren couldn't see the top of them.

Most enchanting of all, twelve torches blazed around the crowd, each with a purple flame that was revealed to be the source of the alluring mist.

It was then that the dark showman took center stage.

"The Tick-Tock Man," Ren whispered.

The magician's coffin stood upright beside

him, with his cane attached to the top of it like a lightning rod.

It looked like he was getting ready to perform a magic trick.

"Welcome to the Big Show! The Halloween Masquerade!" he called out to the crowd of trick-or-treaters, all holding their flickering jack-o'-lanterns. They sat silently, their glazed eyes full of buttery light, still under the enchantment of the mist. "For the past three nights, your bite has granted all your heart's desires. But I know that some of you may regret giving up so many heartbeats in exchange for short-lived thrills. Buyer's remorse, so to speak. But what if I told you there was another deal you could make here tonight—one that would void all the time you've already traded? What if I told you that the bite was just the beginning and that there is a way you would never have to stop trick-or-treating?"

Ren thought of Kip back at Old Manor and was relieved that he was locked safely in their room. He didn't think his little brother would be able to resist the Tick-Tock Man's grand offering.

"If you leave here tonight without taking this final step, you'll remain in your aged forms, and death will come much sooner than it would have otherwise," the magician said. "But if you join us here tonight, you'll never have to know the stench of old age. You can remain young . . . forever."

The gathering of trick-or-treaters listened attentively, their cravings growing, their souls dimming. They had ridden so many rides at the carnival that virtually all of them were now old and withered beneath their masks and costumes.

"Consider this the final altar call for your transformation hour," the magician declared. "For those of you who desire eternal youth, I invite you to the stage to retrieve your soul-clock and feed it to the hub of the wheel. If you deny this gift of salvation, you will leave here tonight with far less than that with which you came. But if you take this last leap, you'll gain everything. The choice is yours."

Even though the sky was grumbling, Ren could hear the coffin onstage ticking as loud as a drum. For a moment, he questioned if it was his own heartbeats he was hearing.

Just then, a peculiar green glow pulsated in the sky, and rain began to pour down over the dark carnival, drenching it with a sick luminescence.

Then . . .

One by one, the trick-or-treaters stood up. Those desiring to bind themselves to the carnival approached the stage, leaving behind their jack-o'-lanterns, pumpkin buckets, and pillowcases full of candy. The few who denied the offer remained sitting in their pews for a moment, then, seeming to find the same strength within themselves that Mrs. Wellshire had conjured long ago, they stood to leave. Ren knew that the ones who had already reached old age would check in to Old Manor the next morning.

This is my chance to find Kip's soul-clock, Ren thought.

He snuck to the back of the line and watched as each trick-or-treater ahead of him opened the coffin door, and their soul-clock mysteriously appeared inside it, hovering in midair. Each clock was a different size and shape and had an unknown amount of heartbeats remaining in it.

Strangest of all, as soon as each person grabbed hold of their soul-clock, marionette strings magically appeared attached to their shoulders from some unseen source high above in the clouds.

It seemed the storm itself was the puppet master.

The strings lifted each convert into the air and dangled them before the hub of the Ferris wheel. Only, it wasn't just a hub. It was a mouth.

If that really is the dark heart of the carnival, then how am I going to get it beyond the boundary? Ren wondered.

He watched as the hub opened its jaws, revealing sharp, salivating fangs. Nearby, the Tick-Tock Man waved his arms as if conducting a macabre symphony. It seemed the world below was the stage for some cosmic battle between good and evil.

An aged boy dressed in a Bigfoot costume tossed his soul-clock into the haunted mouth, and the hub's fangs chewed it while the next trick-or-treater ascended and repeated the ritual. And then another. And another. Until all the clocks had been fed.

All except one, which was still ticking within the coffin.

The Tick-Tock Man noticed one last customer in line wearing a skeleton costume and skull mask.

The magician glanced up at the clock-gauge at the top of his lightning-rod cane.

"It seems there's still one last clock in the coffin," the magician called out to Ren. "Last chance, boy! Only fifteen more minutes until midnight. Time's almost up."

The last clock in the coffin must be Kip's, Ren thought. *This is my chance to get it back.*

Ren slowly approached the coffin beside the Tick-Tock Man, knowing he'd only have one opportunity to grab Kip's clock and destroy the carnival. But just as he was about to open the lid, the magician pulled off Ren's mask.

"I thought I smelled a rat!" the Tick-Tock Man yelled. "Do you have a death wish, boy?"

The other carnies closed in around Ren. The bats circling above descended toward him.

"I'm only here to get my brother's clock back!" Ren shouted.

The Tick-Tock Man laughed.

"I'm afraid it's quite too late for that," he said with an evil smile.

"Give him a refund! Please!" Ren begged.

"There are no refunds at the carnival, boy," the magician replied.

"Wanna bet?" Ren shouted.

Without hesitating, he reached for the coffin door to grab Kip's clock and make a run for it.

But before he could, the Tick-Tock Man opened the ticking coffin at the center of the stage and revealed a man-size mummy standing inside it, already holding Kip's soul-clock.

25

FRIGHT NIGHT

Kip! Ren thought in horror, observing his man-size little brother wrapped in the mummy-gauze that Aunt Winnie had dressed him in earlier that evening. The clock that Kip was holding was strong and daring, a physical representation of his soul.

Kip's eyes were glazed over, as if he was under a spell.

Ren reached for him, but the Tick-Tock Man lifted his hand and zapped Ren with a bolt of purple light. Paralyzed, Ren stood frozen as a statue, unable to move.

"You thought you were clever locking your brother up in your room tonight," the Tick-Tock Man mocked, circling the coffin like a tiger stalking its prey. "But I have many ways to reach those who belong to the carnival."

The mirror, Ren realized. *The Tick-Tock Man brought Kip through the portal!*

"W-why are you doing this?" Ren asked, barely able to move his lips.

"Eternal youth, of course," the Tick-Tock Man explained. "Once your brother feeds his soul-clock to the carnival, he'll belong with us for all of time. I'm grateful to you, Ren, for letting your brother walk right into our tribe. Without you turning your back on him, he never would have known the everlasting thrills of the carnival . . . and we never would have gained his soul."

"I never would have walked away if I had known what would happen!" Ren said.

"Ah, our actions become so clear in retrospect, don't they?" The Tick-Tock Man knocked on the coffin. Kip blinked, revealing there was still some conscious life inside him. Then, slowly, he stepped out of the death-box.

"It's time," the Tick-Tock Man whispered to Kip.

Kip turned his back to Ren and faced the Ferris wheel. Marionette strings instantly attached to Kip's shoulders, lifted him to the hub, and Ren watched as Kip fed his soul-clock to the carnival.

"No!" Ren shouted as Kip descended back to the stage.

"There's nothing you can do now," the Tick-Tock Man said. "Every tick has been sucked into the belly of the carnival and will soon be transferred to our bodies. You see, we feed the carnival, and it feeds us."

Ren remained silent. Helpless. Defeated.

The Tick-Tock Man motioned for the line of trick-or-treaters, no longer attached to the marionette strings, to climb into the twelve carts of the Ferris wheel. Ren watched as Kip and the others handed their special tickets to a middle-aged carnie and climbed on.

A moment later, the Tick-Tock Man pulled the lever.

Ren kept his eyes on Kip as the Ferris wheel began to spin backward.

A flash of lightning struck the clock at the top of the magician's cane, circulating a wave of electric magic into the wheel.

Purple light zapped through each passenger's mask and into their eye sockets. The more lightning that flowed into the magician's cane, the faster the Ferris wheel spun backward.

Thunder rumbled.

Rain bulleted.

Wind whirled.

And the ride rattled.

With each revolution, the tents and rides of the carnival seemed to grow shinier, the food smelled sweeter, and the carnies looked younger.

The backward clock! Ren realized, noticing that the Tick-Tock Man no longer had any gray hair on the sides of his head, and the middle-aged carnie on stage now looked like a teenager. *It's the Ferris wheel! But then . . . what's the heart of the carnival?*

After countless revolutions, Kip and the other costumed trick-or-treaters climbed out of their carts and lined up again on the stage around Ren, forming a circle. Ren couldn't see behind Kip's mask, but he could tell his little brother was back to his normal nine-year-old size.

As soon as Kip and the others stepped back onto the stage, the circle of purple-flame torches surrounding them snuffed out and the jack-o'-lanterns on the pews and midway dimmed.

Finally, the Tick-Tock Man shouted, "Fellow carnies, welcome to an eternity of thrills and pleasures. Now that you are one with the carnival, you may remove your masks!"

Ren watched as Kip removed his mummy wrappings. His face looked young again but paler, and his eyes were . . . solid black.

No! Ren thought, accepting that Kip's soul now fully belonged to the carnival. He looked around at the other trick-or-treaters and realized that they all had black eyes and pale faces as well.

"I said—remove your masks!" the Tick-Tock Man commanded once again.

But . . . they already took them off, Ren thought.

Then, in the eerie glow of the night, he watched as Kip and the others began to peel off their human faces, revealing something unimaginable beneath. . . .

26

FOREVER'S END

Ren cringed at the nightmarish creatures surrounding him. Lightning flashed, illuminating the most hideous faces he had ever seen.

They each had white skin.

Red noses.

Black eyes.

Curly, wiglike hair.

And snakelike fangs.

Clowns! Ren thought in utter horror. *And not just clowns but vampire clowns!*

A flock of bats circled above, and Ren sensed

it was the gang of carnies—ones who had operated rides, sold them food, made them think that the carnival was all fun and pleasures. They screeched in a chorus of darkness, welcoming their new family members.

The rain poured down upon Kip and the sinister cult of clowns, and Ren noticed that the white paint on their faces didn't smear or smudge.

It isn't paint at all, Ren thought. *It's their actual skin.*

The Tick-Tock Man stepped forward and removed his human face like a mask. Beneath it, he looked like the others too, but his eyes seemed darker, his fangs hungrier, and his claws sharper.

Ren realized that the transformed magician looked just like the monster of the darkest dark. The same one he had seen in the mirror maze two nights before.

At the terrified look on Ren's face, the Carnie King said, "What's the matter, boy? Did you really think eternity would come without a price? You should always read the fine print before you sign the dotted line. These faces are the price we pay. But still, you'll grow old and die like all the others. And we'll still be alive."

"You call that being alive?" Ren challenged. "Give me back my brother, or else I'll spend the rest of my life making sure no town anywhere in the world ever lets you in!"

The Tick-Tock Man laughed, and yellow drool fell from his rotted lips.

"You think you're the first to spout empty threats at me during the Feast of Souls? There are far too many towns for you to protect! Villages in jungles and on islands and in secret places you'll never find. But we know them all. We feast on them every seventy-seven years. And there's nothing you can do to stop our eternal cycle."

Ren examined the disfigured shell that was his brother, then peered up at the mouth of the Ferris wheel.

He remembered the words that Zora had spoken: *the bond of love repels evil, but a love-bond broken invites evil in.*

Suddenly . . .

Everything became clear.

"Take my soul instead of his!" Ren shouted.

The Tick-Tock Man laughed.

"Makes no difference to me," the Tick-Tock Man said. "A soul is a soul."

"Then it won't matter if I take his place and you let him go free."

"All right, then," the Tick-Tock Man agreed with a wicked cackle. "Your soul for your brother's. But you pay first. And you'd better hurry before the wheel fully digests his clock and there's no chance of getting it back."

Ren took one final moment to consider the weight of his wager.

"It's a deal, then? I'll receive the bite and feed my clock to the wheel. Then you have to turn my brother back into his normal self and let him go. And you have to promise never to come after him again."

"Deal," the Tick-Tock Man said, putting his hand out for Ren to shake.

The frozen spell released, and Ren shook the magician's hand.

Then, the Carnie King leaned down and

sank his fangs into Ren's forearm. It stung like a bee sting.

Immediately, a soul-clock appeared in Ren's hand. It was ordinary, precise, and in perfect order. There was nothing unusual about it.

The Tick-Tock Man snapped his fingers in command, and the spellbound Kip approached Ren and removed the clock from Ren's hands— the final clock of the night.

"You'll be free soon, Kip," Ren whispered, knowing he might never see his brother again. "Just always remember that I love you."

Kip's black eyes stared back at him, and for a moment, Ren was sure his brother had understood him.

Like a servant, Kip handed Ren's soul-clock to the Tick-Tock Man.

Kip stared at Ren blankly, but Ren soon realized that Kip was slightly nodding toward something, as if trying to give Ren a signal.

Ren glanced over and saw what Kip was wanting him to see.

The clock on the top of the magician's cane,

Ren realized. *All the power of the Ferris wheel is coming through it. The cane clock—it's the heart of the carnival! I have to find a way to move it beyond the boundary!*

Just then, the Tick-Tock Man raised Ren's clock toward the storm.

"Wait," Ren said. "I'll feed it myself."

The Tick-Tock Man grinned and held the clock out for Ren to take. Ren knew he'd only have half a moment to steal the heart of the carnival and destroy it once he retrieved Kip's soul-clock.

He also knew that he would die along with the carnival once he fed his own soul to it.

Ren took his clock back into his hands, and marionette strings attached to his shoulders and lifted him thirty feet in the air to the hub. The voracious fangs salivated, waiting for the final clock of the night.

The Tick-Tock Man stood below, grinning.

"You've already gone this far!" he shouted. "Just go a little farther. There's no way to stop us now!

This is the only way you can save your brother!"

Ren took a deep breath and was just about to feed his soul-clock to the carnival in exchange for his brother's when . . .

A girl's voice called out from beside the stage. "He may not be able to stop you, but I can!"

Ren moved his eyes and saw a vampire clown in a black dress standing there, holding something in her hand.

Zora! Ren thought.

The Tick-Tock Man stepped toward her. "How dare you interrupt the sacred ritual, Zora! What do you think you're doing?"

"What I should have done long ago," she said. "Choosing the other side of the coin."

She flipped a gold token in the air, and it landed in the magician's wretched palm.

Zora then revealed the other thing she was holding. . . .

The glowing heart of the carnival from the top of the magician's cane.

Ren glanced at the coffin and realized the cane was no longer attached to the top of it but was lying broken in two pieces on the stage. Zora had somehow stolen the clock from it while the Tick-Tock Man wasn't looking.

The magician stepped toward her, feigning gentleness, but Ren could tell he was fuming with anger. And fear.

"Dear, dear Zora. Be careful there. I've been a father to you, haven't I? Just like I promised I would be on the night you fed your soul to the carnival," the Tick-Tock Man said, slowly stepping toward her, as if to earn the trust of a nervous animal before snapping its neck. "Isn't that what you wanted more than anything? A father?"

"You took my life from me! And from everyone else!" Zora said, fighting back tears. "I was too young to know the weight of my decision and didn't have parents around to protect me. Everything I've lived for seventy-seven years is a lie—a mask for what I really am. This isn't the way it should be. I should have grown up. I could have fallen in love. I could have had a family. But I sacrificed it all. For this twisted illusion."

The Tick-Tock Man hissed at her like an angry serpent.

"We all choose the illusions we live by, and you chose yours! Now give me back the heart," he replied. "You know the soul-harvest must be finished before midnight or we all starve."

"Let them all go!" Zora shouted. "Or I'll— I'll take the heart of the carnival beyond the boundary!" Ren sensed it wasn't an impulsive threat, but one she had considered a thousand times before.

The Tick-Tock Man shot her a grave look. Kip awaited his next command. Ren watched from above, holding tight to his soul-clock, waiting to see who was going to win this game of chess.

"You wouldn't dare," the Tick-Tock Man said, attempting to call Zora's bluff.

He waited a moment to gauge her next move, then grinned victoriously and turned back toward his army of clowns.

"Goodbye, Ren," Zora called out. "It's time for me to make things right."

Then . . .

Ren watched in shock as Zora held the heart of the carnival close to her chest, sprinted across the midway, disappeared between two tents, and stepped across the forbidden boundary . . .

To forever's end.

27

HEART BROKEN

"NO!" the Tick-Tock Man screamed, running after Zora.

Ren watched from a distance as the heart of the carnival disintegrated and Zora's body morphed into a teenager, then a middle-aged woman, then an old woman with white hair that looked a lot like Mrs. Wellshire's. Then her hair grew past her toes and she was a corpse, lying lifeless on the ground. Last, the corpse turned to dust and blew away in the Hallows' Eve wind with the heart of the carnival just as the banished carnie's remains had done the night before.

The Tick-Tock Man fell to his knees at the carnival boundary and examined the spot where Zora had existed only a moment before. He gazed down in disbelief that both she and the heart of the carnival, his very soul, were gone forever.

Checkmate, Ren thought.

Just then, the marionette strings that were attached to his shoulders disappeared, and he began to fall. He quickly grabbed hold of a bar on the Ferris wheel. Holding on with one hand, he tried to figure out what to do next.

Knowing the Tick-Tock Man wouldn't stay distracted for long, Ren climbed back down the Ferris wheel to the stage below.

The wind howled around him, and a lightning bolt struck the highest cart on the wheel, sending out a thousand fiery sparks into the crowd.

"To the tunnels!" Ren shouted, sprinting across the stage.

He tackled Kip into the burrows beneath the carnival.

The vampire clowns dispersed in every

direction. It looked like a colony of ants after being sprayed with insecticide.

A moment later, the hub of the wheel exploded, blowing up the railing and shocking all its circuits.

The carnival lights dimmed to darkness like veins running cold after a person's heart has stopped beating. Colorful sparks flew out in all directions, showering the ground below. All the while, loud groans and shrieks of a thousand trapped souls pierced Ren's ears.

Violently, the wheel came off the hub and rolled over the nearby tents, making a clear path the width of two school buses. Ren soon realized that the wheel was headed straight toward the magician standing at the edge of the carnival grounds.

The Tick-Tock Man looked up in horror, and right before Ren's eyes, the soulless magician transformed into a bat. He flew straight toward the stage into the empty coffin, and the lid of the death-box slapped shut just before a piece of scaffolding fell upon it, crushing it to pieces.

His final vanishing act, Ren thought, peeking

out from the tunnels.

Just then, a giant twister descended from the clouds and sucked the wheel and the stage up into the sky. It wailed like a train passing through someone's living room, and the booms of thunder shook Ren's eardrums. Green and purple lightning struck all around it in a macabre dance of luminescence. Ren and Kip grabbed hold of a pipe cemented into the ground as everything around them, including the rabid tribe of cackling clowns, was sucked up into the cyclone of terror.

Ren looked up and saw the crazed carnies, the flock of bats, and a swarm of grinning jack-o'-lanterns spinning in a circle, as if riding an invisible carousel up into the storm.

Then, in a single gulp . . .

The entire carnival was consumed.

Suddenly, everything grew quiet. Soft moonlight broke through the dissipating clouds and bathed the world below.

It felt like the carnival had all been a long, terrible nightmare.

Not only that, but it had taken the rotten souls and left behind the innocent ones.

Ren ran to Kip's lifeless body hanging over an underground pipe they had been holding onto. He no longer looked like a clown. He had his real face back, but it didn't look like any life was left in him.

"Kip, please be alive!" Ren cried.

He fell to his knees and held his little brother in his arms.

"Wake up! Please wake up!" Ren pleaded.

Then . . .

A single tear dripped from Ren's cheek and fell upon Kip's forearm.

It washed over the bite mark, melting it completely away.

The bond of love repels evil, but a love-bond broken invites evil in, Ren thought.

Soon, Kip's eyes opened.

"Where am I? Did I survive the Drop of Fear?" he asked Ren.

Ren laughed, deeply glad Kip was back to his usual daring self.

"You survived it all right," he said, then hugged his little brother harder than he ever had in his life. "And next time, I promise to ride it with you."

"And Clowntown?" Kip asked.

"Don't push your luck," Ren replied with a half smirk.

Ren looked around and realized that all the carnies had been taken away in the twister. But the kids who had just fed their soul-clocks to the carnival were no longer clowns. They had their real faces back. Ren even pulled on Kip's cheeks to make sure his face wasn't a mask. He decided there was some small piece of their soul that hadn't been fully digested yet, allowing them to be freed when the carnival was destroyed.

Kip looked down and saw the fresh bite on Ren's arm.

"The bite," Kip whispered, beginning to remember everything. "You—you were going to take my place."

Ren smiled. "Brothers are supposed to

watch out for each other, remember?" he said.

He glanced toward where the carnival boundary had been. A girl's pale ghost was floating there, looking young and free.

"Zora," Ren whispered with profound gratefulness for her sacrifice.

She waved to him.

He waved back.

A moment later, an identical ghost hovered over the nearby field and took her hand.

Mrs. Wellshire, Ren thought in wonder, having not known that, at the very moment he was destroying the heart of the carnival, Mrs. Wellshire had been taking her last breath back in her bed at Old Manor with Aunt Winnie holding her hand.

Mrs. Wellshire smiled at Ren from afar, a deep peace in her misty eyes.

The twins' hearts had the same number of ticks, after all, he thought.

Then the ghosts of the two sisters floated up toward the moon, where they disappeared into the moonlight, to go where all good souls rest.

Ren put his arm around Kip, gladder than ever to have him as his little brother.

"You know," Ren said to Kip. "I think we should hang out more often. No babysitting. No vampire clowns. Just having fun."

"Vampire clowns?" Kip asked.

Ren smiled and hugged Kip again.

And then they both realized that Halloween night was over. At least . . . until next year.

28

A LIFE FULLY LIVED

A few days later, Ren and Kip walked out the front doors of Old Manor, lugging their suitcases behind them. Aunt Winnie was waiting for them on the front steps next to a mushy jack-o'-lantern that hadn't been thrown away yet.

"I've been thinking," she began. "You boys should come visit me every Halloween. I mean, I haven't had so much fun in years."

"Yeah," Ren said. "It was a lot of . . . *fun*."

He and Kip exchanged a knowing smile.

"And did I tell you that Brad at the front desk

asked me to go on a picnic with him next weekend?" Aunt Winnie asked. "He said it was the last thing Mrs. Wellshire told him to do before she passed."

She waved to Brad, who was pushing an old man in a wheelchair through the garden. Brad waved back, smiling a goofy smile and squinting through his thick-lensed glasses.

"That's wonderful," Ren said. "If anyone deserves to be happy, it's you, Aunt Winnie."

He turned his gaze to the graveyard behind them.

"Hold on just a minute," he added, setting his suitcase on the ground. "There's something I need to do before I leave."

Ren walked past the garden and through the iron gates of the graveyard. The air felt cooler, the trees looked barer, and the ground was crunchier, with twice as many leaves. As he ambled through the labyrinth of graves, he read the faded birth days and death dates on each tombstone.

And he realized more than ever that he was alive.

Soon, he stopped at the freshly dug grave at the back of the cemetery, the one still covered with flowers from the funeral the day before.

"Mrs. Wellshire," he said. "I'm glad you're with your sister again. Thank you for teaching me not to be afraid. I promise not to worry too much about getting old and to slow down and enjoy everything along the way. I'll never forget you."

He unfastened his ticking watch from his wrist, tucked it into the ground, and buried it with fresh dirt from Mrs. Wellshire's grave. He imagined her—wherever she was—smiling upon him.

A single red leaf dropped from the tree above and landed on her grave. "Tick tock," Ren whispered. He picked it up and put it in his pocket as a token of remembrance.

Then he turned and walked back toward Aunt Winnie's car.

Without saying anything, Ren grabbed Kip's suitcase and carried it for him, tussling his little brother's hair.

Kip put his hand on Ren's shoulder and

said, "I've been thinking. I'm really sorry about going off on my own the other night. Next time, I promise to listen to you. I know you were just trying to look out for me."

"Better yet," Ren replied, "next time we see a carnival, let's just go to the movies instead."

The brothers laughed as they climbed into the back of Aunt Winnie's car and headed toward the train station.

Ren smiled as he watched Old Manor growing farther into the distance behind them.

He knew that someday he'd be old enough to belong to such a place—hopefully many years from now—and the words written over the image in the rearview mirror confirmed this suspicion. *Objects in the Mirror Are Closer Than They Appear.*

As they drove by the empty field where the carnival had been, Ren thought he smelled the same sweet, haunted scent that had beguiled him on the day he arrived in town.

It was the last remnants of the carnival . . . the soul-harvest.

Most chilling of all, as they approached the train station, Ren swore he heard a wicked cackling in the near distance.

The Tick-Tock Man! he thought, and goose bumps shot up his arm.

But when he looked out the window to the cornfield, all he saw was a lonely scarecrow wearing a tattered black cape.

And so Ren decided it must just be the strange autumn wind.

ACKNOWLEDGMENTS

"I am a part of all that I have met."
—Alfred, Lord Tennyson

There are quite a few people to acknowledge here in this book of the Monsterstreet series:

First of all, my Mom, Dad, Sis—everything I am is because of you, and words can never express the depth of my gratefulness. I can only hope to honor you with the life I live and the works I create.

All my family: Granddad, Grandmom, Pappa Hugg, Mamma Hugg, Lilla, Meemaw, Nanny, GG, Grandmother Hugghins, Marilyn, Steve, Haddie, Jude, Beckett, Uncle Hal, Aunt Cathy, Nicole, Dylan, Aunt Rhonda, Uncle Greg,

Sam, Jake, Trey, Uncle Johnny, Aunt Glynis, Jerod, Chad, Aunt Jodie, Uncle Terry, Natalie, Mitchell, Anna, David, Hannah, David Nevin, Joy, Lukas, Teresa, and Aunt Jan.

Teachers, coaches, mentors, colleagues, and students: Jeanie Johnson, David Vardeman, Pat Vaughn, Lee Carter, Robert Darden, Kevin Reynolds, Ray Bradbury, R.L. Stine, Rikki Coke (Wiethorn), Peggy Jezek, Kathi Couch, Jill Osborne Wilkinson, Marla Jaynes, Karen Deaconson, Su Milam, Karen Copeland, Corrie Dixon, Nancy Evans Hutto, Pam Dominik, Jean Garner, Randy Crawford, Pat Zachry, Eddie Sherman, Scott Copeland, Heidi Kunkel, Brian Boyd, Sherry Rogers, Lisa Osborne, Wes Evans, Betsy Barry, Karen Hix, Sherron Boyd, Mrs. Kahn, Mrs. Turk, Mrs. Schroeder, Mrs. Battle, Mrs. McCracken, Nancy Frame Chiles, Mrs. Adkins, Kim Pearson, Mrs. Harvey, Elaine Spence, Barbara Fulmer, Julie Schrotel, Barbara Belk, Mrs. Reynolds, Vanessa Diffenbaugh, Elisabeth McKetta, Bryan Delaney, Talaya Delaney, Wendy Allman, John Belew, Vicki Klaras, Gery

Greer and Bob Ruddick, Greg Garrett, Chris Seay, Sealy and Matt Yates, David Crowder, Cecile Goyette, Kirby Kim, Mike Simpson, Quinlan Lee, Clay Butler, Mary Darden, Derek Smith, Brian Elliot, Rachel Moore, Naymond Keathley, Steve Sadler, Jimmy and Janet Dorrell, Glenn Blalock, Katie Cook, SJ Murray, Greg Chan, Lorri Shackelford, Tim Fleischer, Byron Weathersbee, Chuck Walker, John Durham, Ron Durham, Bob Johns, Kyle Lake, Kevin Roe, Barby Williams, Nancy Parrish, Joani Livingston, Madeleine Barnett, Diane McDaniel, Beth Hair, Laura Cubos, Sarah Holland, Christe Hancock, Cheryl Cooper, Jeni Smith, Traci Marlin, Jeremy Ferrerro, Maurice and Gloria Walker, Charlotte McDonald, Dana Gietzen, Leighanne Parrish, Heather Helton, Corrie Cubos, all the librarians, teachers, secretaries, students, custodians, and principals at Midway ISD, Waco ISD, Riesel ISD, and Connally ISD, all my apprentices at Moonsung Writing Camp and Camp Imagination, and to my hometown community of Woodway, Texas.

Friends and collaborators: Nathan "Waylon" Jennings, Craig Cunningham, Blake Graham, Susannah Lipsey, Hallie Day, Ali Rodman Wallace, Jered Wilkerson, Brian McDaniel, Meghan Stanley Lynd, Suzanne Hoag Steece, the Jennings family, the Rodman family, the Carter family, all the families of the "Red River Gang," the Cackleberries, the Geib family, Neva Walker and family, Rinky and Hugh Sanders, Clay Rodman, Steven Fischer, Dustin Boyd, Jeff Vander Woude, Randy Stephens, Allen Ferguson, Scott Lynd, Josh Zachry, Scott Crawford, Jourdan Gibson Stewart, Crystal Carter, Kristi Kangas Miller, Taylor Christian, Deanna Dyer Williams, Matt Jennings, Laurie McCool Henderson, Trey Witcher, Genny Pattillo Davis, Brady Williams, Brook Williams Henry, Michael Henry, Jamie Jennings, Jordan Jones, Adrianna Bell Walker, Sarah Rogers Combs, Kayleigh Cunningham, Rich and Megan Roush, Adam Chop, Kimberly Garth Batson, Luke Stanton, Kevin Brown, Britt Knighton, George Cowden, Jenny and Ryan Jamison, Julie Hamilton, Kyle and Emily

Knighton, Ray Small, Jeremy Combs, Mike
Trozzo, Allan Marshall, Coleman Hampton,
Kent Rabalais, Laura Aldridge, Mikel Hat-
field Porter, Edith Reitmeier, Ben Geib, Ashley
Vandiver Dalton, Tamarah Johnson, Amanda
Hutchison Thompson, Morgan McKenzie
Williams, Robbie Phillips, Shane Wilson, J.R.
Fleming, Andy Dollerson, Terry Anderson,
Mary Anzalone, Chris Ermoian, Chris Erlan-
son, Greg Peters, Doreen Ravenscroft, Brooke
Larue Miceli, Emily Spradling Freeman,
Brittany Braden Rowan, Kim Evans Young,
Kellis Gilleland Webb, Lindsay Crawford, April
Carroll Mureen, Rebekah Croft Georges,
Amanda Finnell Brown, Kristen Rash Di Cam-
pli, Clint Sherman, Big Shane Smith, Little
Shane Smith, Allen Childs, Brandon Hodges,
Justin Martin, Eric Lovett, Cody Fredenberg,
Tierre Simmons, Bear King, Brady Lillard,
Charlie Collier, Aaron Hattier, Keith Jordan,
Greg Weghorst, Seth Payne, BJ Carr, Andria
Mullins Scarbrough, Lindsey Kelley Palumbo,
Cayce Connell Bellinger, David Maness, Ryan

Smith, Marc Uptmore, Kelly Maddux McCarver, Robyn Klatt Areheart, Emily Hoyt Crew, Matt Etter, Logan Walter, Jessica Talley, JT Carpenter, Ryan Michaelis, Audrey Malone Andrews, Amy Achor Blankson, Chad Conine, Hart Robinson, Wade Washmon, Clay Gibson, Barrett Hall, Chad Lemons, Les Strech, Marcus Dracos, Tyler Ellis, Taylor Rudd, James Yarborough, Scott Robison, Bert Vandiver, Clark Richardson, Luke Blount, Allan Gipe, Daniel Fahlenkamp, Ben Hogan, Chris Porter, Reid Johnson, Ryan Stanton, Brian Reis, Ty Sprague, Eric Ellis, Jeremy Gann, Jeff Sadler, Ryan Pryor, Jared Ray, Dustin Dickerson, Reed Collins, Ben Marx, Sammy Rajaratnam, Art Wellborn, Cory Ferguson, Jonathan King, Jim King, Anthony Edwards, Craig Nash, Dillon Meek, Jonathan Stringer, the Bode and Moore families, Jackie and Denver Mills, the Warrior Poets, the Wild Hearts, the Barbaric Yawps, the Bangarang Brothers, and all the Sacred Circle guys (CARPE DIEM).

To all the writers, directors, composers,

producers, artists, creators, inventors, poets, and thinkers who have shaped my life, work, and imagination—a list of luminaries which is far too long to mention here.

To Chris Fenoglio, for creating such stunning covers for the Monsterstreet series. It's safe to say your illustrations pass the ultimate test: they would have made me want to pick up the books when I was a boy! Thank you for lending your incredible talent and imagination to this project.

To the Stimola Literary Studio Family: Erica Rand Silverman, Adriana Stimola, Peter Ryan, Allison Remcheck, and all my fellow authors who are lucky enough to call the Stimola Literary Studio their home.

To the entire HarperCollins publishing family and Katherine Tegen family: Katherine Tegen, David Curtis, Erin Fitzsimmons, Jon Howard, Robby Imfeld, Haley George, and Tanu Srivastava.

To my amazing agent, Rosemary Stimola, who plucked me out of obscurity, remained faithful to this project over the course of not just months but years, and who sets the highest standard of integrity within the wondrous world of children's publishing. I can't tell you how deeply grateful I am for all that you have done for me.

And to my extraordinary editor, Ben Rosenthal. From our very first conversation reminiscing about 1980s movies, I felt in my gut that you were a kindred spirit. Our collaboration on the Monsterstreet series has been one of the greatest joys and adventures of my life, and it's an enormous honor to get to share this journey with you. Thank you for all your guidance, encouragement, and optimism along the way . . . you've been a fantastic captain of this ship!

To my wife and best friend, Rebekah . . . no words can ever tell you how grateful I am for the thousands of hours you've spent reading rough drafts, listening to unpolished ideas, and offering warm, thoughtful encouragement every step of the way. These books wouldn't exist without you, and I'm so glad I get to share this journey and all others by your side.

And lastly, to my most cherished treasures, my precious daughters, Lily Belle and Poet Eve: it is the greatest joy of my life to watch you gaze upon the world with wonder and tell us what you see. May stories always enchant you, and may you tell your own stories someday.

KEEP READING FOR A SNEAK PEEK AT ANOTHER
CHILLING MONSTERSTREET ADVENTURE

NO SERVICE

The dirt road twisted through the forest like a snake, but the scrawny boy in the passenger seat didn't notice. His shaggy hair and brown eyes were veiled by a red hoodie as he stared down at his iPad, annihilating monsters on some faraway planet.

Suddenly, the cell bars at the top of the screen vanished, and the game froze.

"No service?" The boy shook the device, trying to wake the dead.

"You'll survive for a couple of days, Max," his mother said, driving their blue minivan deeper into the woods. "When I was twelve, we didn't have all those distractions—we played outside. It will just take some time to get used to being away from the city."

Max sank into his seat and sighed.

He looked out his window, and saw the tall, prickly pine trees for the first time. On the side of the road, he glimpsed a rusted metal sign that read, *Now Entering Wolf County. Population 781.* Oddly, the number "781" had been crossed out with red spray paint, and "634" had been written in its place.

"Creepyville," Max mumbled, then turned to his mom. "Do I really have to stay out here the whole weekend?"

It was more of a plea than a question.

"We've already been over this, honey," his mother replied. "I swear, you're just like your father—always questioning things. That's what made him a good scientist, I suppose."

"But I've never even met these people. And now you want me to stay with them by myself for three days?"

"You've met them before. You just don't remember," she said. "In fact, we lived out here for a while when you were a baby. Before—"

She paused, and there was an awkward moment of silence. Max knew she was about to refer to his father's accidental death, but it was something she rarely said aloud. He had asked her about it more times than he could count, but she always found a way to change the subject before he could get any real answers. In fact, he hardly knew anything about his father.

"Believe me, Max, this is the last place on earth I want to be," his mother said, tapping the steering wheel. She had been acting strangely toward him the past few days. "If you want to know the truth, your gramps and grammy wrote me a letter on your birthday asking for you to come stay with them this weekend. They seemed rather urgent about it. Said they have some things of your father's that they want to pass down to you. It was supposed to be a surprise."

Max still wasn't convinced.

"Why haven't they ever come to our house? And why is this the first time we've gone to see them?"

His mother took a deep breath.

"You're getting older now, and I think it's important for you to spend some time with your father's side of the family. After he died out here, I swore never to come back. But—"

"Wait," Max interrupted. "Dad's accident happened here? At the place you're taking me?"

His mother nodded.

Max sat back in his seat and gazed forward. It was the only clue she had ever given him about his father's death.

"Mom?" he began.

"Yes, honey?"

"When are you going to tell me what really happened to Dad?"

The question was simple, but it ran deep and wide inside of him, like a story with no ending.

Max had no memories of his father. When other kids' dads visited them at school, he

4

pretended not to care that his own dad could never come. When other kids played catch with their dads at the park or in the yard, he turned his head so that he wouldn't have to feel the pain of missing his own father. And yet, he had never known *why* his dad wasn't there. The only thing he possessed that had once belonged to his father was the faded red hoodie he was wearing now—the hoodie his grandparents had sent to him a few days before on his twelfth birthday.

Max played with the zipper as he watched the shadows of trees creep over his mom's face. She glanced over at him and opened her mouth to speak. Max was sure that he was finally about to get some answers. But her eyes dimmed. Her lips sealed. And her gaze turned forward.

"I've already told you. Your father died in a hunting accident when you were a baby," she said.

But Max sensed there was more she wasn't telling him. And he wanted to know the truth.

Read the

MONSTERSTREET

series by

J. H. REYNOLDS

"Fast, funny, frightening—and filled with shocks and surprises.
These books are my kind of fun. I want to *live* on Monsterstreet!"

—R.L. Stine, author of the Goosebumps series

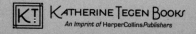

KATHERINE TEGEN BOOKS
An Imprint of HarperCollins Publishers

www.harpercollinschildrens.com